STAROAMER—

A name out of history, an immense generation ship, it had been built by humans more than five centuries ago. Then, only a few years after its launching, it was gone, lost in the depths of space.

Now Quarnian's syron talents brought her and her companions on a journey to uncharted starways, straight to the airlock of the legendary, ill-fated *Staroamer*. Once inside the vast, echoing chambers of the mystery ship, she would uncover the shocking fate of Earth's bravest explorers ... and discover the awesome secret that would threaten the freedom she held so dear ...

STAROAMER'S FATE

Chuck Rothman

POPULAR LIBRARY

An Imprint of Warner Books, Inc.

A Warner Communications Company

POPULAR LIBRARY EDITION

Copyright © 1986 by Chuck Rothman
All rights reserved.

Popular Library® and Questar® are registered trademarks
of Warner Books, Inc.

Cover art by Enric

Popular Library books are published by
Warner Books, Inc.
666 Fifth Avenue
New York, N.Y. 10103

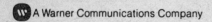 A Warner Communications Company

Printed in the United States of America

First Printing: January, 1986

10 9 8 7 6 5 4 3 2 1

To Susan, who believed

Chapter One

New Wichatah City is laid out in a neat, logical pattern, alphabetically from east to west, numerically from north to south, all in little neat squares a hundred meters on a side. Its inhabitants reflected the design—there wasn't a decent bar open after the twentieth hour.

Quarnian had found out the hard way. Her current stop was a dingy little box, ill-lit, smelling of stale native beer, and filled with failed farmers and congenital alcoholics. Its patrons all wore a standard two days' growth of beard, as a mark of recognition, a uniform, unchanged since the dark ages on Earth.

Quarnian took another sip of the greenish liquid from the glass in front of her. It was beginning to taste almost tolerable, so she figured that she must be pretty far gone. If this was real tola wine, she was on the planetary council. It was probably just green watercolors mixed with turpentine. She'd probably go blind if she had another glass.

She asked for another glass.

The bartender frowned. "You've been having a lot of those, my lady."

"I'm not your . . ." Quarnian stopped. There was no reason to be antagonistic; the title was customary here. "I don't want to talk," she muttered. "Just give me another."

"I'm sorry, but I can't. We'll be closing soon."

Quarnian studied his face. He was lying. It was just a polite way of shutting her off.

She shrugged. There were other bars.

Quarnian tripped as she got off the stool, grabbing the mulchwood edge of the bar to keep from grinding her clothes into the damp and muddy floor. She pulled herself upright and, moving carefully, made a sine curve for the door.

Two men began to follow.

The fresh air of the street revived her a little, and she knew she could walk as far as the next watering place. She turned her sharp indigo-blue eyes upward as though trying to get her bearings from the stars. New Wichatah's three tiny moons made an equilateral triangle above her head; local astrologers considered this a good-luck sign. She tried to trace out the constellations. She picked out Sirius, as bright in the sky as Venus is from Earth. The Wichatans called its constellation "The Coathanger." Accurate, but also indicative of their imagination.

She started down the street, thinking there had to be some place open nearby. Her long brown hair, thin as cobwebs, had fallen into her face. She should get it cut someday, maybe have her head shaved (that was the style on Radis). It might be an improvement.

But, she then reflected, she never really was happy with the way she looked. People had called her attractive, but she always found it hard to believe. Her face seemed nothing special — oval shaped, with a small nose and mouth. Nothing to be ashamed of, but certainly not stunning. She was slender enough, she supposed, and she kept herself in good physical condition. Someone had even called her graceful once.

She noticed the sound of a pair of footsteps behind her. They were speeding up, tap-tapping on the stone pavement, and they were obviously going to overtake her. Someone had chosen her to be a victim. Her spacer's clothes probably made them think she had money. She idly wondered what they had in mind.

"Excuse me, lady." The voice was like a ratchet. Quarnian decided she wanted to know what the face attached to it looked like. She turned; it was a disappointment. Some people's faces didn't match their voices; it was never more true than now.

This man was just slightly taller than she, with a gentle-looking face and a smooth cheek that looked as if it had never been touched by a razor. He wore a battered brown overcoat, showing its age by a few half-hidden frayed spots.

His companion was barely more than a meter and a half tall. His face was a disaster area: a round moon, with craters to match, topped off by a bulbous nose decorated with a wart. A screaming red scar puckered along his right cheek. He hid in the shadows, tiny eyes glittering in the streetlights.

"Yes?" Quarnian asked.

"We heard what you said. We thought you were looking for another place."

And they knew of one; Quarnian was sure of that. Her drink would be delicious — and laced with a sedative. Then, who knew—robbery, rape. She had heard Borna was interested in human women for slaves. She'd soon disappear like the legendary *Staroamer*.

It sounded like fun, but not tonight. Instinctively, she reached for her neck to draw out her pendant. She only touched skin.

Quarnian giggled. She was drinking to forget and she had forgotten. "I'll be glad to go with you, Mr. . . ."

"Smith," the ratchet-voiced man said.

Quarnian smiled. "Of course. I'll be glad to go with you and Hugo."

"Name's Bruce," the short man mumbled.

"Mine's Quarnian." She tried to curtsy, but only fell to the pavement.

"Let me help you." Smith reached out to grab her arm.

She pulled away from him, studying his face, trying to read it through the haze of alcohol. Smith wasn't going to resort to violence just yet; he'd wait until the proper time came. She was safe for the moment.

She let them bring her to her feet.

The two of them led her through the streets. Quarnian began to feel a bit more lucid; she gave Bruce a quick read.

She was surprised at what she saw: a curious mixture of childishness and suppressed violence, of fear and mistrust. He only worked with Smith because he had to. She felt sorry for him and she decided not to kill him.

The roadway slowly darkened; if Quarnian had had any sense, she would have turned back. But she didn't care. The drinks had emboldened her and, besides, she was used to trusting her luck.

"Here we are," Smith said.

The doorway was mulchwood, discolored by grime, and there was a darkened spot where years of oily hands had pressed. As she looked, the door jerked open. Quarnian saw a few dingy tables visible in the murky room and a man leading a woman up a flight of stairs in the back.

Quarnian felt indignant. If they were going to sell her into prostitution, they should at least have the decency to take her to a classier place than this.

"Quarnian! I've been looking all over for you!"

Smith turned to see who had spoken. Quarnian didn't have to; she knew Rex Carlssen's voice.

"You're coming with me," Rex said.

"The lady's with us," Smith said, ungentlemanly, as he glared at the newcomer.

Bruce stepped out of the way of the other two men. Quarnian thought they looked like the griffs on Odin, huffing and puffing in ritual battle. But with griffs, one would back down, and it wasn't likely that was going to happen here.

"I don't want to fight," Rex said, his tone denying the words. "Quarnian's my partner."

"She was alone," Smith said, his hand moving slowly into his pocket. Quarnian could tell he was reaching for a beamgun, but he wasn't going to fire it just yet.

"You know who that is? That's Quarnian Dow. She's a syron."

Smith's face showed a hint of fear as he glanced at her. Bruce moved even further away.

"You're lying," Smith said. "Where's her necklace?"

"Yes, Rex," Quarnian said, her tongue flagging loose from alcohol. "Where is it?"

Rex flinched at her tone. "Are you sure you want . . . ?"

"Sure. What the frast. Go ahead."

Rex studied her for a moment, then shrugged. "I sold it."

Smith didn't believe him, Quarnian realized. He was going to use his weapon.

She had determined his weak spot while they had walked here. Her finger reached just below his right rib and pressed in a precisely-timed pattern.

Smith shrieked and tried to whirl away. His right knee buckled under him. It was only a matter of time. He realized it and tried to speak, but only saliva came from his mouth, saliva mixed with dull gurgles.

Quarnian waited; Smith's eyes closed.

"For star's sake, you didn't have to . . ."

She ignored Rex and turned to Bruce. "You."

He cowered farther from her, as though even her words could kill. "Don't . . ."

"Want a job?"

Bruce could only cringe.

"Want a job?"

Bruce had some control over himself now. He nodded warily, as though the wrong answer would be his last.

"Fine. Come to the spaceport tomorrow at the fifteenth hour. The *Wreckless*."

"*Wreckless*," he repeated.

"Let's go, Rex." The alcohol was wearing off; she never could stay drunk for long, and without looking back to see if he was following, she set off.

He huffed to get near her. "Why'd you kill him?"

"For star's sake, I didn't. He wasn't worth the effort. He should wake up in a few hours; he'll just have a limp for a few weeks."

He studied her silently for a few minutes as they walked. You didn't have to be a syron to know what he was thinking. It annoyed her.

"Look, Rex, I don't like killing. You think it's scary that I can know everything about you? That I can kill with a touch? Well, it's scary for me, too."

She could tell he didn't understand, and she gave up trying to talk about it.

"Are you serious about that other one?"

They had reached one of the more hospitable sections of the city. "Bruce? Very."

"But why? You can never tell if—"

"I can." Quarnian felt the need to change the subject. "How much did you get for the pendant?"

"Only a hundred trents." He sounded apologetic. "There isn't much demand for—"

"I know that." She felt annoyed. So little! And giving it up had been one of the hardest things she had done since she had completed her Training.

"We'll need a lot more."

They had reached the edge of the spaceport, and Quarnian was tired of conversation. "You let me worry about that," she said. She'd explain later.

Chapter Two

The next morning brought a change of perspective. Quarnian woke up with her head clear, without a trace of a hangover. The sun was shining through the small round window of her cabin, leaving an oval of light on the floor. It almost made her feel cheerful. Her gloominess seemed almost gone. Pawning her pendant was pawning a symbol, and it was always a mistake to put too much faith in symbols.

She wondered what Rex thought about her little performance last night. They had only met the morning before. She had just set foot in New Wichatah City, and was looking around, trying to figure out what had impelled her to catch the first ship there. On impulse, she had wandered around the spaceport. The pilots watched her warily as she strolled. She could almost smell their curiosity; the rumor of what she was had evidently preceded her.

She had been drawn to the *Wreckless*. It was a standard subcee freighter, a bit worn out, with signs of rust on her struts and large black stains of spilled fuel along its sides. Squares of metal showed where tiles had fallen from its heat shield. It had probably been secondhand when Rex had got it. She didn't even have to look inside to know the layout: a main control room, three cabins for the pilot and any passengers he wanted to carry, and a large cargo area.

Without thinking why, she had gone inside, entering as though it were her own ship. The interior was less decrepit than the hull, but still showed signs of wear. A man wearing the most respectable of gray suits was talking to Rex, his eyes like those of a shark.

"I just need a little more time," Rex was saying as she entered.

The man shook his head. "The bank has been more than patient with you. You're eight months behind on your ship's mortgage, and I'm afraid we're now forced to foreclose."

"But I need—"

"You'll get your money," Quarnian said.

The man in the suit turned, surprised. "You have it?"

Quarnian barely had enough for a cup of coffee. "Not right now. But you'll get it in five days."

The man looked amused. "Oh? Do you expect to come into a fortune?"

She ignored the sarcasm and held up her pendant. "Recognize this?"

The man's eyes almost bulged. Quarnian smiled. The pendant really wasn't much to look at: a twelve-pointed star of gold leaf, with alternating long and short points, on an oval piece of obsidian as black as space. Hers was a bit dirty and stained from constant wear, but it was enough to identify her as a gold-star syron.

"You'll have the money in five days," Quarnian had said.

The banker left quickly, mumbling that her word made fine collateral and looking as if he'd agree to anything she said. It was a mixture of fear, respect, and the knowledge that syrons can always make money quickly. And, if she failed, it wouldn't matter to him. He'd still get the *Wreckless*—just a few days later than planned.

Quarnian turned to Rex. "I'll be needing your ship once I bail you out," she said, not realizing that that was her plan until the words popped out of her mouth. "You can pilot for me in return. Any objections?"

Rex's face had shown some of the fearful respect that the

other man had, but as he looked at her, his expression turned into a smile. Part of it, she realized, was the knowledge that a syron could be a gold mine. Part of it was something else, something you didn't have to be a syron to read. Any woman could probably tell he was making certain very definite plans for the two of them. "No objection at all," Rex grinned.

So now they were a team, and the idea of having an ally was almost novel.

Quarnian stopped daydreaming and began to get dressed. They had a lot to do today.

Rex had breakfast ready for her: pancakes with sweet-wood syrup. It was probably the last of his supplies, but she knew he was trying to soften her up.

"What exactly do you have in mind?" Rex asked as she finished.

Quarnian took one last bite, savoring its tangy sweetness. "Can you guess?" She smiled.

"Well . . ."

"We need money, right? A hundred trents won't do a thing to keep the bank off your tail. So . . . ?"

He eyed her warily, as though her coaxing tone was some sort of trick. Quarnian didn't blame him; she *had* been rather brusque with him from the start. It was the best way to keep him from getting too many ideas.

She could see he was about to tell her his answer, but she beat him to it. "Right. We make a few strategic bets."

Rex looked dazed, then grinned. "I wish you wouldn't do that."

"Can't help it. Besides, how else would you know I was for real?"

"But there's no casino here. And we can't get to Gemma until . . ."

Quarnian shook her head. "No casinos. They'd never let me in; their security computers have every syron in the universe on file. We have to go to the racetrack."

Rex rubbed his hands together. "Now you're talking. I'm a pretty good handicapper myself and we can—"

"I hold the money," Quarnian said sharply. "I make the bets."

Rex's smile evaporated. "Sorry, I—"

"You'll just have to remember who's boss around here."
Rex nodded.

Quarnian studied him closely. He was a handsome man,
and he knew it, with wavy black hair and deep brown eyes
that probably helped to make him a very successful woman-
izer. He was a little taller than she was, and years of hauling
cargo on and off the *Wreckless* had developed him quite
nicely.

But why had she chosen *him*? She looked for clues. He
was smart, certainly, with an ability to follow orders that
was rare in a space jockey. He was also an odd mixture of
caution and impatience—but what advantage would that
be?

She gave up. Everything would be revealed eventually. It
took patience to be a syron, and you usually got the answers,
but it always took time.

She checked the time. "Let's get going."

Racing had followed the colonies all over the universe;
even a place like New Wichatah, which put a premium on
its straightlaced appearance, had been unable to resist, as its
farmers succumbed to the urge to see which animal was
fastest and to make a little bet on the side.

Wichatah Park was a small, no-nonsense structure of
whitewashed truwood. Open only one day a week, it
attracted the curious from all over the planet. The stands
were already almost filled when Quarnian and Rex got
there. She spotted a couple of seats by the turn. They
weren't great, but they weren't there for the view.

Quarnian looked over her program. There were eight
races scheduled, for different distances and for different
classes of toffils. She read the names in the first race, but
nothing struck her eye.

"Well?" Rex asked.

"Give me a minute."

The toffils were parading in front of the grandstand.
Horses rarely left Earth, so settlers made do with the local
wildlife. A toffil may have been fast, but it looked like a
joke. Its multicolored plumage, a cross between feathers and

hair, covered a scrawny body that seemed to be all legs and thighs. Quarnian was reminded of a toy she had had years ago, a bird that dipped its head in and out of a glass of water. Each toffil had a driver behind it, seated awkwardly on a two-wheeled cart.

"Any decision?"

"Yes. We skip this one."

Rex seemed about to grumble, but she cut him short before he could get out a word. "We're here to make money, not to have fun."

Rex grinned. "I thought making money *was* fun."

She had to smile back. "You're right. But I have no idea who's going to win."

"But you can tell—"

"Let's get one thing straight. I can't read minds and I can't tell the future."

Rex nodded.

She knew he didn't believe her; the legends were too persuasive. Everyone thought of syrons as superbeings, able to see the future and look into people's minds as easily as reading a book. It just wasn't true. A syron was specially trained to use his or her natural intuition. You realized what people were thinking by their facial expressions and body language; you learned how to listen to your hunches. Yes, there was probably some telepathy involved (that was what differentiated Quarnian from a red-star syron who was only able to perform party tricks), but no one knew how to turn it on and off, or even what caused it. It was only in the past fifty years that scientists began to believe that there might be something to telepathy after all.

And it wasn't all fun, either. Sometimes your hunches forced you to do things you didn't want to, things that made Quarian shudder whenever she thought about them. You no longer had control over your life; you learned to live with the idea, but it still remained a dull ache in the back of your mind.

Quarnian shook her head and went back to concentrating on the program.

By the third race, Rex began to get nervous. Quarnian tried not to let it bother her as she studied the list.

"There," she said. "That one. *Forella's Dream*. Put twenty on it."

"Twenty? Why not all?"

"Put twenty—oh, never mind. I'll do it myself." Better not to tell him that she wasn't always right. Being thought infallible has its uses; people are less likely to question your requests.

She made the bet and returned to her seat just as the race went off.

The toffil started slowly, as though biding its time. Quarnian didn't begin to feel nervous until it reached the top of the stretch, sixth in a field of nine. Not now, she thought. As she urged it onward, it began to make its move, slowly gaining ground on the leaders. . . .

It finished fourth.

Quarnian swore, but not as loudly as Rex.

"What happened?" he demanded.

"I was wrong," she said, quickly and quietly, hoping the matter would be dropped.

It wasn't. Rex looked at her, his face showing amazement, his voice showing scorn. "Wrong? It can't be. A full-scale gold-star syron like you could never—"

"Quiet," Quarnian snapped.

"No. You've been pushing me around with that star ever since I agreed to help you. Do this, do that—and promising it would be all worth my while because you're a goddamn syron. I'm getting sick of it."

Several people were looking at them; Quarnian felt her face become warm. "I'm sorry," she said, quietly and simply. He was right. She *had* been ordering him around shamelessly; she could have been more subtle. "I haven't been thinking."

Rex glared at her a little bit less. "All right. Just stop treating me as worthless."

Quarnian nodded. "Agreed."

"Fine. Now let's look at the next race."

Quarnian looked down the list; one name caught her eye and wouldn't let go. She pointed. "That one. Roman Star."

Rex looked over her shoulder. "Long odds. How much do we bet?"

"Everything."

"Everything? But—"

"Everything." Quarnian said the word firmly, but without ordering. She felt a solid confidence as it left her lips. This was the real thing.

Rex caught her tone; his protest never materialized. Shaking his head, he went to place the bet.

"Drivers up," came the cry as he returned with the tickets. Quarnian didn't look at him; her eyes were glued to the toffils as they stood behind the starting gate. She picked out Roman Star. It was a pleasant pale blue. Her favorite color; it might bring her luck.

"The field is off."

The eight entries began to run. Roman Star moved in quickly along the rail, its driver holding the reins tightly.

Quarnian felt herself clutching the arm of her seat.

The field raced forward. Roman Star stayed in the middle of the pack, biding its time. No attempt to move forward, even in response to Quarnian's urging.

At the top of the stretch, it pulled out and began to charge.

It passed the others slowly, one at a time, fourth to third to second. It pulled even with the leader. . . .

But a third toffil had pulled up on the far outside. It was moving faster than Roman Star, inching up to challenge for the lead. There was no doubt it would pass Roman Star; Quarnian could only hope the finish line would intervene in time.

It didn't. Roman Star lost by a beak.

For the first time in years, Quarnian felt tears. Her pendant and her money were gone, and all for nothing. She battered her hands against the arms of her seat, trying to either break wood or bones.

In the midst of her frustration, she realized that Rex hadn't said anything. She turned reluctantly to face his scorn; it would be punishment enough.

He was grinning. "Quite a display. I wonder what you would have done if you had lost."

"What do you mean?"

"I didn't quite trust you. I bet the toffil to show. We're still in the running."

So that was how his caution could help her!

Quarnian had the sudden urge to kiss him. She started to lean forward, but stopped herself in time. Men were always falling for her. Once they got over their fear, the mystery and excitement seemed to bring out their hormones, and she didn't want to open that can of worms.

Rex had begun to lean, too. Her sudden change caught him off guard.

An awkward silence fell. Quarnian wondered if she should explain. She couldn't afford any intimacy or emotional closeness; her life was too unsettled for that. She was always darting around the universe, following her hunches with no idea why, and she usually had to act alone. There was barely any room for friendship, and she'd have to make that clear.

Rex spoke before she had to. "Better cash these," he mumbled. "It's not enough to outfit the ship, but I have a feeling your luck will change for the next race."

She smiled. "You're playing hunches; that's supposed to be *my* job."

While he was gone, she scanned the program, feeling more confident now. Once again, a name leaped out at her. "Rob's Rocket," she told Rex when he returned. "This time, bet it to win. All of it."

Rex shook his head as he left. "I'll bet to win. But only half of it."

Quarnian decided not to argue.

"Eight thousand trents," Quarnian counted. "Plus change. Is that enough?"

"It's plenty. I can get the bank off my back, fuel up, and even make repairs."

"Repairs? You didn't say anything about repairs."

"You never asked. You were too busy giving orders."

His tone held no malice. Quarnian smiled in response to his grin. Underneath, he was a decent sort. She might even get to like him, . . . and she'd have to be careful of that.

The grandstand was nearly empty as the two of them

made their way into the streets of the city. The streetlights, replicas of antique electric ones, which were part of the natives' efforts to be more earthlike than Earth, were just coming on, glowing gently as they warmed up. There was still about a half hour to darkness, but the Wichatans took no chances on the dark.

"Back to the ship?" Rex asked.

Quarnian shook her head. "I want to make one detour. Take me to where you sold my pendant."

The pawnshop was a respectable place, with none of the seediness Quarnian had expected. Over the door was the traditional dollar sign, with the name "Rycroft's" underneath it in elegant calligraphy.

A man in his fifties, his hair growing sparsely on his head, sat behind the counter, reading the news terminal. He had a graying wisp of a mustache that at first glance seemed to be a smudge of dirt on his upper lip. His clothes were ragged, yet Quarnian could sense an understated elegance in his manner. She knew he had to be Rycroft.

"Greetings," he said, bowing his head. "What can I do to serve you?"

Quarnian pointed at Rex. "You must remember my friend from yesterday. I want to buy back what he sold you."

Rycroft nodded. "I thought you'd be coming for it today, what with the race meeting this afternoon. I even stayed open a little late. I know a lot about syrons." He stuck out his hand.

Quarnian looked at it. What was he doing?

"It's an old custom here," Rycroft explained. "Dates back from Earth, I hear. You grasp hands."

"What's it supposed to do?" Rex asked.

The storekeeper shrugged. "I don't know. A sign of friendship, I guess. You don't have to, if you don't . . ."

"I'll be glad to," Quarnian said, regaining her composure. It wasn't so much the custom that had shocked her—she now recalled reading about it once—but it was the way the man understood her thoughts. He might have had the Training himself. She looked at him closely, trying to see.

He nodded. "Many years ago, of course. Silver star."

Quarnian raised an eyebrow.

"I got tired of it."

She nodded, understanding the undertones in his expression. Syrons quit for a variety of reasons. Sometimes their talent faded, other times they just found it impossible to live with themselves. But it was hard to quit. She hoped that when her time came, she'd be able to walk away from it the way he had.

"I hope you will."

"What are you two—?" began Rex.

"Nothing," Quarnian said, waving his words away before he could finish them. "How much do you want for my pendant?"

"Just what I paid your friend."

"Oh, come on. You're entitled to something for your trouble."

"No trouble at all."

"How much do you want?"

"Quarnian!" Rex said. "Don't argue with the man. Money's not easy to come by these days."

Rycroft looked at Quarnian with renewed respect. "Quarnian Dow?"

She didn't even have to nod; he knew he had hit the target. "Then I'm doubly honored." He reached underneath the counter and pulled out a small box. "Here. No charge."

Her pendant was inside. The golden star shone at her from an obsidian sky, the border between black and gold sharp and well-defined. It almost seemed to glow, as though it were brand-new—or lovingly polished.

She felt embarrassed. "Please, let me—"

"No. And good luck."

Quarnian sighed. The matter was closed. She'd have to figure out a way to send him the money later. "Thank you," she said as humbly as she could, and motioned for Rex to leave.

"What is it you've done?" Rex asked as they followed the beeline street to the spaceport. "He acts like you're a big deal."

"Some other time," Quarnian said quickly. She never liked to talk about her exploits.

They walked in silence to the *Wreckless*. Quarnian wondered how long the repairs would take. There was an itchy feeling in the back of her mind, urging her to get going. No telling what a long delay would do to her.

As they reached the ship, a small dark figure popped out of the shadows.

Quarnian instantly shifted to the ready, preparing to defend herself. It took her a second to recognize the scar on his cheek. "Bruce?"

"You're late," he grunted, stepping forward. "Been here since fifteen." A livid bruise stained the underside of his left eye and Quarnian could see flecks of blood on the edges of his nostrils.

"I'm sorry," she said. "We were delayed." She paused for a moment, then went on. "What happened to you?"

"Nothing," Bruce mumbled.

"What happened?" Quarnian asked, gently insistent.

Bruce looked at her cautiously for several moments. "My friend."

"Smith?"

Bruce nodded sullenly. "He was mad. Can't stay with him anymore. Have no—" he broke off, stopping himself from saying anything more. "Is the job still open?"

Quarnian knew the rest of his unfinished sentence: Bruce had no place else to go. "Yes," she said. "I think we can still use you." Her instincts were buzzing as she said the words; they were *right*. "Come in the ship; there's an extra cabin for you."

Rex glared at her as she said it, but her answering look kept him quiet. The three of them entered the ship, ready for a chance to recover from the day.

Chapter Three

"I don't think we should trust him," Rex said the next day. "Why do you want him along?"

Quarnian pointed out the viewport to Bruce; he was busily seeing to the loading of the ship. "Look at him. You really think he's going to do anything to us?"

"Appearances can be—"

"Not to me."

Rex no longer seemed so upset when she interrupted him. "You don't seem to worry about anything. One of these days . . ."

"You're right. One of these days I'm going to get myself killed. But look at him. This is his big chance; he's not going to blow it."

"His big chance to steal a ship. And look at the expense of getting his suit. The little runt can't fit into a standard model."

Quarnian sighed. "I don't want to talk about it anymore."

"I just don't like him with us. He'll get in the way."

Quarnian looked at him closely. There was something in the way he said it . . . Sure. Rex still considered her a potential sex partner. Evidently she hadn't done enough to let him know that that was out of the question. "In what way? What do you mean?" she asked innocently, trying to get him to commit himself.

"Well, Quarnian, you *are* a good-looking woman. I thought maybe you and I might—"

"Rex, I'm not interested in going to bed with you."

"That's all right. I understand. In fact, I respect you for telling me. I realize you have the right to make your own decision on the matter." He smiled charmingly at her.

She sighed. "How often does that line succeed?"

Rex turned red. "Line? I don't know what—"

"How often?"

Rex's eyes turned deckward. "Often enough," he mumbled.

"Let's get one thing straight. This trip is strictly business."

"Sure, but—"

"I want to be sure you understand that. If you don't get the message—well, you saw what I did to Bruce's friend."

She could see Rex understood the threat. "Now, Quarn, there's no need—"

"I just wanted to make that clear. Oh, and don't call me 'Quarn.' I hate that nickname; it sounds like an alien disease."

"All right, Quarnian."

There was a sullen tone in the words. She knew she'd have to diffuse it. "Cheer up. You're not stuck with me forever."

"Thank God," Rex said, a tiny smile creeping onto his lips.

She went on, cheering him up and feeding his ego. It was no trick to say what he wanted to hear, just another part of the Training. Understanding a person's emotions gave you a key to his character, a handle to get him to do whatever you wanted. Quarnian was an expert at it and, in a case like this, she didn't have any qualms about using her skill. In only a few minutes, she had put him into a more cheerful mood.

It was suddenly broken by the sound of shouting outside.

They raced down the steps of the *Wreckless*. Bruce was wrestling in the dirt with one of the laborers. He was getting

pummeled; the other man outweighed him by twenty kilos.
Work had stopped as people jockeyed for a front-row seat.

Quarnian pushed her way to the battle. Rex had already
grabbed hold of the larger combatant; she grabbed Bruce
and pulled him out of the way.

He struggled against her. "Let go!"

She ignored his demand. "What happened here?"

There was a sudden silence; all eyes fell on her and her
pendant. Even Bruce stopped his struggling, as though he
suddenly realized it was a syron that held him.

"Well?"

Rex kicked his prisoner's ankle. "You heard her."

The man looked up, sullen and fearful. "Nothing," he
mumbled.

"Caught him," Bruce said. "Stole from ship."

"He's lying," the man said as Rex ran his hands into his
pockets. He found a beamgun stashed inside his pants and
held it up.

"That's mine," the man said, without a trace of embarrassment. "I bought it a few days ago."

Quarnian looked at his face. "You're lying," she said.
"We'll—"

A man stepped forward from the crowd. "You cannot call
my brother, Brinn, a liar, even if you are a syron. The gun is
his; I was with him when he bought it."

"I saw it yesterday!" another voice shouted. "Brinn
showed it to me!"

"Apologize!" someone else shouted.

Rex walked over to Quarnian, holding the beamgun in his
hand. "What now?" he whispered.

She shrugged. She didn't like the way they were sticking
together. "It's our gun."

"You're right. But there may be other guns out there. If
we're not careful, they'll be fired at us."

Quarnian didn't need the warning. The universe was filled
with anti-syronism; they were just too different and frightening. She might be able to hold the crowd off, but it
wouldn't help anything in the long run and someone might
get hurt. "What do you suggest?"

"Give him back the gun; we can get another. And apologize. We'll be leaving soon, anyway."

Bruce shook his head roughly. "Called me a liar, too."

"You just might have to let it pass," Quarnian muttered as she thought.

Bruce could barely suppress his emotion. "Must pay!"

"There are more important things right now," Quarnian said coldly. She stepped out of the conference. "Brinn!" she shouted. "I have examined the gun. My assistant has lied; it isn't ours."

"Lady!"

Quarnian gave Rex a glance; he knew enough to keep Bruce from saying anything more.

"It's not ours," she repeated. "It's an inferior model; we only use the best."

Brinn tensed; she went on before he could say anything. "I am sorry I called you a liar; I trusted my assistant. I humbly apologize." She walked over to him and handed him the gun.

He snatched it and disappeared to join his companions.

She and Rex helped Bruce to the ship. His eye was rapidly blackening and a trickle of blood mixed with the dirt beneath his nose. He didn't say anything.

"Frast!" Quarnian suddenly cursed when they were safely inside. "Why did I give him that gun?"

Bruce had disappeared into the head to clean up. "What do you mean?" Rex asked.

"I don't understand why I did it. It *seemed* the right thing to do, but I know Brinn isn't planning to use it to help anyone but himself."

Rex smiled. "I pulled out the power pack and smashed the crystal. If he could afford to fix it, he wouldn't have needed to steal it. You didn't think I gave him a working model, do you?"

Quarnian relaxed. She should have known better than to doubt her instincts, but it was sometimes hard to remember that when your actions didn't seem to make sense. "I suppose I did know, only I didn't."

"I don't understand."

"Neither do I, really, but it'll take too long to explain. Go down and make sure they finish loading us properly. And carry a beamgun, so they'll be less interested in stealing things."

Rex hurried down.

Quarnian sat at the control couch and sighed. It had been a close call; she had been considering trying to fight them all off.

She smiled bitterly to herself. A choice in the matter? Ridiculous. She had long ago stopped believing in free will.

She was only a puppet, dancing to an invisible and unknowable master. Total intuition sounded nice to those who didn't have it; the ability to read other people's feelings seemed like a useful tool. She had thought so, once. . . .

She remembered her excitement in the beginning; it seemed eons ago. She had grown up on Krote, a wet mudball planet where the biggest excitement was watching the equivalent of snails mating. She had dreamed of adventure.

Quarnian smiled wryly.

Even from the beginning, she knew she was different. She remembered when she was seven, coming home from school the day before her birthday and *knowing* that there was a surprise party waiting behind the front door.

Her father ran a provision store and had expected her to do the same. She had helped out as best she could, but it was boring, even though she did have a certain knack for anticipating who might be thinking of shoplifting and being there before it happened.

It continued through her teens, knowing what boys had crushes on her, and when it was safe to give in to them. She remembered the time she had passed up a ride from her friends and discovered that their hovercraft crashed not ten minutes later.

But she never realized what she was until the day a goldstar syron wandered into her father's store. He was a white-haired man in his thirties with an irritated look on his face, as though he had come there against his will. He took one look at Quarnian and pointed. "You," he had said, and she knew exactly what he meant. She applied to the Syron Institute the next day, spending nearly a week's pay for the FTL post. The answer came back a month later: she had been acepted. It meant four years on Earth and a way to avoid being stuck in a dank swamp for the rest of her life.

Her parents had objected, until she showed them the part where the Institute had offered to pay her expenses. Then they brimmed over with pride, as though it were their idea from the start. Not that she herself was blasé about it; she bored all her friends with her bragging.

The first year at the Institute had been exciting, too— learning the Training, discovering how to truly see others, to understand their motives and the undertones hidden beneath their words. She was quick to learn, but she didn't consider the reason why.

Then she was called to the dean's office. She had been terrified, afraid she was going to be asked to leave.

But the news had seemed unbelievably good: gold-star potential. Then Dean Wylen explained just what that meant. Being pulled along by unseen forces, knowing your life wasn't really your own.

She didn't believe it. All she knew was the comic books and tridees, where a gold-star syron could do anything she wanted.

By the time she understood what she was getting into, it was already too late.

It had been nine years now since she had been able to really enjoy herself, to do something without worrying whether her decisions were her own or not, of having to find reasons for unreasonable actions.

If she had only known, she never would have . . .

Again a bitter smile crossed her face. She knew it wouldn't have made any difference.

She looked up. Bruce was emerging from the head. The blood and grime had been washed off, but his left eye had nearly swollen shut. He looked even uglier than usual.

He saw her glance. "Lady," he said, gruff and pleading at the same time, "why?"

"Why? Why what?"

"You called me liar."

Quarnian smiled. "Don't worry about that. I know you're not. I just had to say you were."

"To others!"

She didn't understand the accusation in his tone. Concentrating on his face, she tried to get a feel for what was upsetting him.

Nothing; too many conflicting emotions canceled themselves out. All she could get was a general impression of agitation.

"Yes," she said slowly, trying to choose the right words, "but why are you so upset?"

"Will be ruined."

"Ruined?" Quarnian had a picture of him as he was when she first met him. "How could you be any more . . . ?"

"You don't understand." Bruce turned to his cabin, showing no inclination toward explaining.

"Wait a minute. Bruce, I'd like to know—"

He glared at her like a wild animal; she knew it would be better to change the subject. "I want to know your last name. In all the confusion, I forgot to ask."

His eyes focused on the steel of the deck. "D'Arcangelis," he mumbled, just loudly enough for her to make out. Then he vanished into his cabin like a child escaping the consequences of an unpleasant truth.

"D'Arcangelis," Quarnian whispered to herself. Of the archangel. Or—listening more to sounds than etymology—dark angel. She wondered which would be an accurate description.

Chapter Four

The *Wreckless* was ready four days later.

Quarnian felt it was about time. Her impatience continued to grow; every second that passed made her more nervous. Rex bore the brunt of her questions and urgings. Several times he thought she might be rushing him a bit too much, but she never communicated that concern to him.

Bruce didn't communicate with her at all.

Finally, everything was done. Quarnian watched as Rex went through the final check before lift-off. He knew what he was doing; his hands were moving over the controls as though they had an intelligence of their own. Another confirmation: she had chosen well.

"Tell Bruce we're ready," Rex told her.

Quarnian got up and knocked on Bruce's cabin. He had rarely left there since their last conversation.

She knocked; no answer. She shouted the message through the door.

"Still moping," she reported when she resumed her seat.

"I'm not surprised," Rex said, not looking up from his work. "I just hope he's got enough sense to strap in."

"Wait a minute. You know why he's doing this?"

"Sure." He pulled down a mike. "Control, this is *Wreckless*. We're ready to lift off."

"Then tell me—"

"Roger, *Wreckless*. Your window's ready. Start countdown in one minute."

Quarnian knew her answer would have to wait. She watched, fascinated, as Rex manipulated the controls, checking dials, flipping switches, reporting data. It had been years since she had traveled by slowship; she tried to remember the last time she had had to sit through this type of takeoff.

The count reached zero.

At first, all Quarnian could feel was the vibration massaging her. For several moments, she thought there had been a malfunction, then she realized she was beginning to feel heavier. A leaden feeling grew in her wrists and ankles, increasing slowly but relentlessly.

Warpships did everything they could to reduce acceleration, but the *Wreckless* was not first-class travel. She had never liked fighting gee.

The ship continued to rise; the daylight in the viewport now became stars as they passed out of the atmosphere.

The acceleration was beginning to hurt, as though someone were trying to pull the bones through her body. Quarnian realized she was gritting her teeth.

She cursed to herself. She was out of shape.

Her eyes shut; she realized she was about to black out. She fought against it, hating her weakness. She was acting like a first timer. She turned her head painfully toward Rex to see if he had noticed it.

His eyes were closed, too.

Quarnian fought against the sudden feeling of panic. Something was wrong. The burn was going on too long.

She lifted an arm; it felt as if it were tied down. She'd have to cut the engines herself, then bring Rex back to his senses to plot a course. She reached out for a duplicate switch in front of her.

It took all her strength to make any progress. Her hand crept toward the switch. She felt dizzy, about to lose control any minute. If that happened . . . well, they'd run out of fuel eventually. By then, the acceleration might have killed them all.

She could no longer see; her eyelids were attached to lead weights. Her hand closed on something. Praying it was the cutoff, she pulled just as the blackness descended.

She woke to a gentle shaking.

"Quarnian, are you all right?"

She opened her eyes. Rex was looking down at her as he floated above her. His face was stoic, but she could read the fear beneath it. He had had a good scare.

"Fine," she said, trying to move from the couch. Her bones ached, but she would recover. Nothing seemed broken. "What went wrong?"

"I don't know. I hit the frasted cutoff and nothing happened. I think the switch jammed. If I get hold of that bastard who sold it to me, I'll turn him into toffil food." His voice became less filled with disgust. "It's a good thing you—"

"How do we stand?" Quarnian always tried to head off compliments when she could see them coming; she called it her Lone Ranger Syndrome. "Any damage?"

"We've used a lot of fuel; it might cause trouble landing if we have to maneuver too much. Otherwise we're OK."

"How's Bruce?"

Rex turned slightly red. "I . . ."

"You didn't see. Go find out."

He disappeared behind her and she took a deep breath. She didn't like what had happened. It was a close call; she could see it in Rex's reaction.

She began to wish she really were clairvoyant. Then she might have some idea about what was in store. If she had come so close to disaster so soon, what might happen later? Generally, a syron's feelings didn't let him be killed, but sometimes one did die while following a hunch. Afterward, it usually turned out that the sacrifice was necessary. Not much of a consolation to the person who made it, but great for the reputation of the Training.

Rex returned from his mission, gliding along in

weightlessness like a bat. "He's fine. Didn't even lose consciousness. The little creep is tough."

"He talked to you?"

"Sure. Two syllables at a time, of course, but that's normal. Won't he talk to you?"

She shook her head. "He's upset about something. Something about that problem with the gun."

"When you called him a liar? You didn't smooth it over?"

"I tried, but . . ."

"Probably didn't even know what to do. I thought you syrons could tell everything."

Quarnian felt her face grow hot; she wasn't sure if it was with anger or embarrassment. "We can't—"

"Don't you know *anything* about New Wichatah?"

"The guides said—"

"Forget them. They're put out by the Chamber of Commerce. You think they're going to tell you the real story? They pretend that everything's perfect—but New Wichatah's just like any other planet. There are people who don't fit in, who don't want to work picking fruit all their lives. Or who aren't able to. Some of them become criminals.

"The trouble is, no one wants to admit they exist. The planetary council's made up of rich farmers and ranchers who never spend much time in the city, anyway. They think the problem will go away if they ignore it."

"So everyone runs wild?" Quarnian asked.

"Of course not. The crooks aren't stupid. They know the more noise they make, the more dangerous it'll be for them. They stay in the city and only prey on those who haven't the power to complain. It's become an entire underground culture."

Quarnian could sense deep bitterness in his words. "Were you part—?"

"Not me. Strictly middle-class all the way; my folks worked in computer maintenance." Rex grinned. "How do you think I was able to scrape up enough to make a down payment on the *Wreckless*? But that doesn't mean I didn't see what was going on. There are two New Wichatahs out there: the part the guides talk about, the colony that Lucas

Trent envisioned when he founded the place—peaceful, bucolic, with no troublemakers—and the underside.

"That's a different story. Even the guides try to steer you away from certain parts of the city. You can imagine what those thugs might have planned for you."

Quarnian nodded.

"Those people live by their own rules. Sort of a code. Very stupid and rigid, but one too powerful for a person like Bruce to ignore. They're a lot different from our own laws— and much less forgiving.

"You insulted Bruce; a liar is the second worse thing you could call him. According to his rules, the insult has to be avenged. Or else he's a coward. That's the worst."

Quarnian understood. She remembered how furious the laborer had been over her accusation.

"Bruce didn't dare challenge you. He was shamed—and in front of witnesses. He may not be able to show his face in the city again."

"Oh, come on. . . . "

"Sure. Might makes right with those people—and they won't forget. Bruce will eventually be forced to fight. Sooner or later, he'll lose."

Quarnian felt a shiver of shame.

"He won't be able to become much more than he was, either. The cream makes sure that the milk doesn't rise."

Quarnian rarely asked others for advice, but she knew she was in over her head. "What should I do?"

"Show him it doesn't matter. Promise to pay his way to another world."

It sounded right; she went to restore harmony.

"All right," Rex said, "you're paying for all this. Any idea of which way you want to go?"

Quarnian shrugged. "Away from New Wichatah, I guess."

"Nothing more specific?"

"Away from New Wichatah," Quarnian repeated. Suddenly a thought occurred to her. "In the direction of Earth."

Rex shook his head. "That's a long way from here; this isn't a warship, you know."

"Rex . . ."

"I know. I'm just the hired man. Ours not to reason why and all that."

"Try to save fuel."

Rex nodded. "My thought exactly. We won't bother spinning the ship for gravity; it takes more fuel to maneuver if we don't have to compensate for that. It's standard procedure. Can you take zero gee?"

"I'm taking it now."

"Fine. Now strap in. We're going to have to maneuver a little. I promise it'll be more gentle this time."

"Promise?" Quarnian smiled at his tone.

Rex shrugged. "Keep your hand on the cutoff if you want. But I always keep my promises."

Quarnian nodded. "Wait. Shouldn't I tell Bruce?"

"Heard," came the voice behind her.

Quarnian's head swiveled. Bruce was swimming awkwardly behind her, as much out of his element as a whale on Sirius IV. Once again, she tried to read his expression and failed.

"He keeps promises, lady," Bruce said. "Do you?"

The sarcasm in his voice forced her to act. She put her hand on her pendant and drew it out to let Bruce know she was grasping it. "Bruce," she said, slowly and solemnly, "I swear by the star to find you a new world to live on. Away from New Wichatah." She let the pendant go. "Does that satisfy you?"

Bruce's eyes widened momentarily, then froze back into his stony expression. "Maybe. If that's worth anything." With as much dignity as he could project, he floated toward his cabin.

Quarnian felt herself turning red; an oath by the syron's star had the force of natural law. Everyone knew that. Bruce had only said it to upset her; she knew her oath had had the desired effect.

Chapter Five

Three weeks into the trip, Quarnian was ready to scream, and she was the calmest of the crew.

There's not much to do, stuck in a small metal box with no idea where you're going, Quarnian thought as she watched Rex and Bruce glare at each other. Their antagonism was becoming more and more apparent. She had taken some time to trim off most of her hair; it was the high point of the voyage.

She knew it was her fault. Her choice of crew hadn't taken compatibility into account; Rex and Bruce had the wrong chemistry to be able to do more than just tolerate each other, and her presence made matters worse. There was a sexual tension in the air, playing across the faces of the two men as they looked at her. She knew Bruce would suppress it—she doubted he ever had much contact with women, anyway. But Rex was another matter. A woman was a challenge to him; he resented Bruce's presence. Despite Quarnian's full-time efforts keeping Rex in line, she knew he thought Bruce was all that stood in the way of a weightless idyll.

The situation quickly neared the flash point.

"Look," she said, breaking the sinister silence, "let's face it. We're bored. We've got to find something to do or we'll end up killing each other."

Bruce nodded slowly and sullenly.

"Any suggestions?" Rex asked.

Quarnian shrugged. "At the very least, we can talk."

Rex snorted at the idea. "About what?"

"I don't know."

"Lady," Bruce said quietly. "Talk about Tlebor."

Rex stared at the scar-faced man. "Tlebor? What the hell's—?"

"You know about Tlebor?" Quarnian asked, impressed by Bruce's knowledge.

"Recognized your name."

"How? Who told you about me?"

"A man. He lends money. He told once."

"You still haven't said . . ." Rex began.

"One of my adventures," Quarnian said with distaste. She hated the term. They never seemed adventurous while they were happening, but somehow they gained in luster as they traveled around. "I don't like to talk about them."

"Why not?" Bruce asked.

"Because . . ." She stopped. Yes, it might be an answer, something to relieve the tension. "All right, I'll tell. But on one condition: we take turns."

"Take turns?" Rex asked.

"Sure. Tell us something you did once—or something you've heard. It doesn't matter. We'll swap tales around the campfire."

Rex shrugged. "All right. You first."

Quarnian took a deep breath. She wasn't sure how to begin; she had never talked much about the subject. "It was eight years ago. I had just finished my Training. I had a hunch. . . . " She smiled wryly. "I guess I was still enthusiastic about them. I was proud to be a syron. Too proud.

"I had my own ship in those days and I set out—"

Bruce interrupted. "You stole a dreamstone."

Quarnian sighed. "Yes. It was on Nisus and belonged to . . ." She felt her throat close up, but went on despite it. "To Henri Zwiko. I—"

"The Zwiko dreamstone!" Rex said.

Quarnian looked at him. "Am I telling the story or are you?"

"I just remembered hearing something about it. It's the biggest one ever found, isn't it?"

"At the time."

"But how'd you get it from him? The security around it must have been ferocious."

"I don't want to talk about it." The memory was painful and filled her with anger. It was the first time she had discovered the degradation her hunches could lead her to. She still wasn't used to it, and she knew she never would be. "Trade secret," she said, smiling gently to hide her feelings. "Anyway, we took off from Nisus with police from about six planets on our tail."

"We?" Rex asked.

"A pilot I hired," she said hurriedly. She didn't like to think about Guy Turnbull; she had almost made the mistake of falling in love with him. "It was pretty close, but we managed to get to Tlebor before they caught us. The riln were there, and they needed the dreamstone."

"The riln? Don't they make dreamstones?" Rex asked.

"Yes. That's why they're worth a fraction of what they used to be." She smiled. "Only a fraction of a fortune. I'm the one to blame for that. But the riln needed that particular dreamstone because their sun was about to go nova."

"And you stopped it," Bruce whispered. "Didn't you, lady?"

Quarnian forced a laugh. "Don't be ridiculous. That's only a rumor. The riln needed the dreamstone as a sort of a lens to focus energy to save their sun. Dreamstones feed on brain waves; that's why you can't keep your eyes away from them. I was just the messenger."

Bruce frowned. She could tell he didn't believe her. The rumor that she had stopped a star from exploding had gained too much strength over the years. At first, she hadn't bothered to deny it, thinking it meant nothing. But she noticed people's fear. Fear of the supernatural, fear of unlimited power. And fear built too many walls. Now it was too late to undo the legend; she could now only hope that there were those who hadn't heard it. "Once they saved themselves," she went on, "they rewarded me lavishly. I was able to give Zwiko three dreamstones to pay for rental of his, so no one complained."

"Lady," Bruce said very quietly, "how do you do it? How did you know where to go?"

A tired ache dulled her emotions. "I don't know, Bruce. No one does, not even Alan Syron when he invented the whole thing."

"That's ridiculous," Rex said. "The Institute—"

"They know how to teach the Training, that's all. It's not all that complicated. You're just taught to read facial expressions and body language, and to learn to listen to things you used to ignore before. It's just a matter of becoming sensitive."

"You mean I could—?"

"You could learn it all, but you'd never get a gold star. Red, blue, maybe even green. If you had the potential to be anything more, you'd already be a syron. You're born a silver or gold star, and those with the ability just naturally gravitate to the Institute.

"But no one knows why it works."

She took a deep breath to clear the bitterness from her voice. She doubted they understood, but it didn't matter. "Now," she said as cheerfully as she could, "how about you, Rex?"

"I can't top yours."

"Don't even try. Just tell us about something you did."

"Well . . ." Rex was silent for a moment, then a grin filled his face. "I used to have this friend, Lorne Walters. Lorne had the wildest imagination. He'd do the most outrageous things—like when he kidnapped the head of the planetary council."

"What?" Quarnian and Bruce asked, almost in unison.

"Not the real council," Rex added quickly. "It was one of those mock councils for high school students. Lorne locked the guy who was president and a bunch of counselors in a room and began making demands—the abolition of Tuesdays, fewer tridee reruns, a ban on colored underwear—that sort of thing."

"What happened?" Quarnian asked.

"Well, he was grabbing everyone who came by. Pretty soon the kidnapped outnumbered the kidnappers. They escaped. None of them would identify Lorne, so the whole group had to listen to a speech about the danger of making a mockery of a solemn process." Rex grinned as though the lecture was the funniest part of the story.

"I wasn't a part of that, but a few months later Lorne had this other idea. We got dressed up in tuxedoes—they're these fancy outfits, kind of a jacket and frilly shirt. They look bizarre, but they were popular on Earth centuries ago and are still the height of fashion in some circles. Don't ask me where Lorne got them. He wouldn't tell me.

"We also took along these toy blasters. They were about a meter long and made of cheap plastic, but from a distance they looked pretty much like the real thing."

Rex's eyes twinkled in enjoyment as he went on. "Lorne and I went to the Starlight Room. At the time, it was the fanciest place in the city. No farmers, just politicians, lawyers, and the richest of tourists. Lorne told me to keep my mouth shut and follow his lead.

"We stepped inside." Rex gestured in front of him. "There was a sort of platform by the door so that everyone could see us. Lorne began to look around the room, as though he were looking for someone." Rex demonstrated, his head slowly turning, his eyes narrowed and staring.

"You should have seen how quickly the room got quiet. People were gaping at us as though their eyes were about to pop. I remember one woman . . ." Rex snorted out a laugh. "Her mouth was wide open. She had a mouthful of sauerkraut at the time.

"Finally, after about half a minute of this, Lorne turned to me and said, just loud enough for everyone to hear, 'He's not here.' We turned and walked out without looking back."

Quarnian began to smile along with Rex. She could imagine the face, the puzzled conversations after they left.

"So that's it," Rex said. "No world-saver, but I still have a lot of fun thinking about it."

"Where's your friend now?" Quarnian asked.

Rex shrugged. "In New Wichatah. He's a minister. He doesn't like to talk about his past."

Quarnian laughed. "No, I guess not." She faced Bruce. "Your turn."

He frowned. "Don't like to talk."

"Let's go," she teased. "It was your idea."

Bruce appeared reluctant, then shrugged. "This isn't true. It's an old song." He opened his mouth and, in a cracked and broken voice filled with uncertainty, began to warble a tune.

> The *Staroamer* was a pretty ship
> As big as the eye could see.
> It vanished as it reached for the stars
> And took my friends from me.

Bruce's voice slowly became stronger as he reached the chorus of the ancient ballad.

> Set sail for *alpha centauri,*
> Set sail four years and ten.
> The *Staroamer* set sail one day
> And never came back again.
> The *Staroamer* had my brother aboard,
> My brother and my friend.
> We listen to the radio
> But hear no word from them.

Bruce repeated the chorus, his voice taking on the added coloration of emotion, as though he became less fearful of scorn for his singing.

> One day they'll find the *Staroamer,*
> Its crew now turned to dust,
> The ship a wrecked and broken hulk,
> The dream all turned to rust.

His voice had taken on an aching sweetness as he launched into the chorus one more time.

> Set sail for *Alpha Centauri*,
> Set sail four years and ten.
> The *Staroamer* set sail one day
> And never came back again.

Bruce fell silent apologetically and pushed off for his cabin.

Quarnian watched him go. The song had stirred something in her, much more than its lyrics and sad tune warranted. "The *Staroamer*," she whispered.

Rex shook his head. "He sure can sing. I never would have expected it of the little runt."

Quarnian ignored him. The feeling was stronger, a hunch about to burst from her mind to her lips. "The *Staroamer*," she repeated, more positively this time.

"What about it?"

"That's what we're going to find."

Rex looked at her as though she had grown an extra head. "You're crazy. People have been searching for the *Staroamer* ever since it vanished. When something that big disappears, it practically becomes a legend. Frast, it is a legend; you heard Bruce. I even think there's some sort of big reward. What makes you think we're going to find it?"

"We are, Rex. I know we are."

"Quarnian, in case you forgot, the *Staroamer* was heading for *Alpha Centauri*. That's light-years from here."

"It *has* been five centuries," Quarnian reminded him.

"Yes, but that's not even in the right direction. The—"

"It's out there, Rex," Quarnian said flatly. "It's headed our way. Look, Rex, I can't explain how I know, but I do. It's like when you feel something's not right with the *Wreckless*—or that a particular woman might be willing to go to bed with you. It's a feeling, almost as though I can sense it out there."

Rex stared at her for a moment. "You know, you scare me."

Quarnian laughed. "I scare a lot of people—myself included. It's part of the price you pay."

Chapter Six

"There's something out there," Rex announced a week later.

Quarnian felt his excitement hidden under the words. "What?"

"I can't tell yet. The radar only shows—"

"Is it the *Staroamer*?"

He smiled. "It could be. It looks like you're right again."

She felt a bit of relief; she began to smile back. "You should have known better than to doubt me."

"I don't want you to become unbearable. I'm going to be stuck with you until we're done with this adventure."

"I'm not too bad to be with."

Rex shook his head in mock dismay. "I can see it's too late. You *are* unbearable. I should lock you in your cabin."

"I'd like to see you try." Quarnian was enjoying the verbal duel. "You couldn't have found the *Staroamer* if you—"

"The *Staroamer*?"

Embarrassed, Quarnian turned to face Bruce. He had silently joined them, floating as though he were born without weight. The weeks without gravity had taught him a lot.

"Is it the *Staroamer*?" he asked.

"It could be," Quarnian said. She tried to read his expression; as usual, he gave little away.

Bruce just looked back at her.

"I guess everyone'll be happy to know what really happened to it," Rex said, oppressed by the long pause.

"Know the *Staroamer*," Bruce said. "Read . . ." He paused, obviously embarrassed by the admission.

His group looks down on readers, Quarnian realized. "There's nothing wrong with that. How much do you know?"

"Everything," Bruce mumbled.

"Everything?" Rex asked, scorn in his voice.

Bruce looked at him defiantly. "Everything." He turned to Quarnian and his eyes grew soft, as though he were begging her to believe him. "Saw the movie eight times. *Legend of the Staroamer*. With Judy Deutscher, Clay Adams, Terrence Swift, and James Hill. Not easy—had to sneak in. And had—" He broke off as though afraid to go on with the sentence. "Had other things," he muttered, his face reddening. "Please, lady," he went on. "Believe me."

Quarnian believed him. No wonder she had brought him along. "All right, Bruce. You can give us lessons."

He sneered at her and she immediately knew her mistake: lessons were almost as bad as reading. Bruce floated away, heading for the safety of his cabin.

"How long before we reach it?" Quarnian asked.

Rex answered with a shrug. "Two, maybe three days before we're near enough to dock. But there's going to be a problem."

"What?"

"It's going awfully fast. It'll take a lot of power to match its orbit."

She finished his thought for him. "And we're short of fuel. Do we have enough to do it?"

"I think so. But we're not going to have enough left to land back on New Wichatah." He looked at her closely, testing her reaction as he said the words. "It might not be a problem—we can radio for help as soon as we're near. But if we have to maneuver too much on our way back, or if any hitches come up . . ." He shrugged.

Quarnian knew better than to show him any doubt. "We'll get back." She smiled, knowing he'd react best to a light touch. "Wasn't I right about the ship being out here? Don't worry about a thing—I'm feeling particularly infallible today."

He smiled back at her and began punching buttons on the control panel. "Just planning the course."

Quarnian said nothing. She was manipulating him again; it bothered her. She kept telling herself that everyone was manipulated, one way or another. It wasn't always a consolation.

"God, you look gloomy, Quarnian. You're not the most enjoyable passenger I've had in here."

She smiled at the way he said it. "Who was?"

"A woman I was taking to Gemma. She had just left her boyfriend—an unpleasant fellow as she described him—and needed some comforting. She and I—"

"I get the idea."

"Seriously, Quarnian, I'd like to know what you expect to find there." He tossed his head in the direction of the viewport.

"I don't—"

"And for star's sake, don't tell me you don't know. Take a guess."

"Wouldn't you rather ask Bruce? He's the expert."

Rex shook his head. "No evasions. Besides, unless he's singing, he's as enlightening as a burned-out light bulb. Speculate."

"Well . . ." Quarnian sat back, trying to sort out the theories she had read over the years. The *Staroamer*'s disappearance was one of the great mysteries of the universe, and ideas about what happened to it were as common as snow on Argus IV. It was the first ship to head for another star, a giant generation ship filled with Earth's most adventurous crew. And it had just vanished, its radio messages coming to a sudden halt. There had been no hint of trouble.

Over the years, there had been thousands of guesses, three films, two plays (not counting the musical version), and volumes of speculation, songs, poetry, and stories. The most pessimistic ones had now been proven wrong; Quarnian tried to sort through everything else. "There may be nothing," she said, picking the first theory to come to mind. "Everyone might have died centuries ago."

"Do you think that's likely?"

She liked the way he got to the heart of the matter. "No. The *Staroamer* was self-contained. There's no reason why it couldn't have gone on for another five hundred years."

"Unless there was some disaster."

"Make up your mind which side you're going to be on. Besides, I don't think we'd be here if that were the case. So the crew is probably alive."

Rex took a look at the readings on his computer screen. "So we're on a rescue mission."

"Possibly. Except . . ."

He looked up at her. "You think they might have reverted to barbarism."

Quarnian felt a chill, the paranoia that only a syron can feel when he or she is suddenly read by an outsider. "How do you know that?" she asked coldly.

If Rex was puzzled by her tone, he gave no sign. "Frast, everyone's heard of that. It was probably old hat when the *Staroamer* was first lost. I don't think it's likely, though."

"Why's that?"

"Same argument you made. If we came here for a reason, it wasn't to rescue a bunch of people who are little better than cavemen." He tapped several keys on the computer. "Well, whatever's there, we'll be ready for the history books. I'm sure I even heard somewhere that there was a reward." He frowned as he looked at the display.

"What is it?"

"That thing's going awfully fast. I don't know. . . . "

"Can you match it?"

"At top speed, yes. Just barely. Although—"

"You let me worry about the fuel. We'll get back."

Rex began adjusting the controls of the *Wreckless*. "I must be going crazy," he said, shaking his head slowly. "I believe you."

That's one of us, Quarnian thought.

Two days later, Rex confirmed it: it was the *Staroamer*.

Chapter Seven

The *Staroamer* loomed over them like a giant tin can. Rex and Quarnian searched for a sign of activity, a place to dock. Bruce was behind them, saying nothing.

"I think I see . . ." Rex began. "No, just a reflection."

"How about near the front?" Quarnian suggested, her voice hushed. The ship was enormous, the largest human structure ever. Room for a crew of nearly ten thousand, with space for equipment, livestock, and gardens.

"The bow," Rex corrected. "And I'm heading that way now."

The ship hung above them like a small planet. It wasn't turning. Not a good sign—its crew didn't have gravity. Could people survive that way, continue to stay viable and sane for such a long time? Did the ship have any power at all?

"There!" Bruce said suddenly.

His voice startled her; she had forgotten he was behind her. "What?"

"A light." He pointed his arm.

She strained to see. Nothing . . . no, something caught her eye. A quick glint that disappeared as the *Wreckless* moved by. She couldn't tell if it was a reflection or something more. "Maybe," she said. "If we could only find a place to dock."

"There's one," Bruce answered. "Central section, sternward of the ID numbers."

Rex looked at him, his face skeptical. "I didn't see any . . ."

"Bruce's our expert," Quarnian said. "Give it a try."

They found the numbers, each numeral as large as the *Wreckless* itself. At their end was a black spot, a deformed period.

"That's it," Bruce said.

Quarnian smiled. "Rex, is it big enough to fit through?"

Rex reluctantly nodded, as though he hated to admit Bruce had been right. "Big enough for two of us. Don't worry about me; I can thread this needle."

Almost effortlessly, the ship plunged into the hole.

Rex moved forward cautiously. The passage was dim, without any starlight to grant illumination. Eventually, with the help of the ship's searchlight, they were able to make out features.

The entrance widened into a hangar. Five shuttleship berths were visible in the searchlight, all empty. Quarnian had the feeling they had been unused for centuries.

There was something threatening about that. Where could the ships have gone? The *Staroamer*'s course seemed to be a direct line from Earth; there was no stopping points along the way.

Did they try to get back to Earth? If so, why hadn't anyone heard about them?

Rex brought the *Wreckless* into one of the empty berths and cut the rockets. "This is the best I can do; the *Wreckless* isn't quite the right fit. We're probably a meter or two from their airlock."

Quarnian could see he was nervous about the missing shuttleships, too. "I want to take a look inside. Will we be safe here?"

Rex shrugged. "Safe enough. I've got grapples out; even if we manage to spin the *Staroamer*, we'll be OK."

"We won't try that."

"I didn't really think so. I'm getting used to weightlessness. I also wanted us to be secure so that I could go along."

Quarnian was puzzled. "I had expected you would."

"I wasn't sure. You're the leader and Bruce is the expert." He said the last word with only a faint hint of sarcasm. "That would leave me holding the fort."

"We'll all go," Quarnian said firmly. "We're all here for a reason. We'll find out what it is when we get aboard."

They suited up silently. Quarnian didn't like vacuum suits; she thought she looked ridiculous in them. She knew there was a reason for coloring them bright yellow—easier to see—but she felt like she was going to a masquerade in a canary suit.

Still, there wasn't much choice; they had to pass through a vacuum to get in the *Staroamer*, even if there was still air left inside. She pulled the suit on over her clothes; its light but strong plastic formed a loose shell around her. At least it didn't hamper her movements; the older suits were as bulky as medieval armor.

She sealed the helmet over her head, reflecting how the name was a poor description for the clear plastic bubble that protected her. It was soft and flexible, held rigid by internal air pressure when in space. When it wasn't needed, it could be folded flat and put into a side pocket of the suit.

She had just picked up her beamgun when Rex's voice came over the suit radio. "All ready?"

She said she was; Bruce just grunted in the affirmative.

They entered the airlock and waited for it to cycle.

The outer door swung open, revealing another two meters away; Rex had docked as perfectly as promised. He shot a magnetic grapple and pulled himself over. Quarnian and Bruce followed.

"Now comes the hard part," Rex said as they reached the lock. It was just a door set in the hull of the ship; a switch panel stood to the right of it. None of its lights were glowing. Rex reached out and flipped one of the switches.

Nothing happened.

Quarnian waited to be sure, but the door just wasn't going to open. "What does that mean?" she asked.

Rex shrugged. "Could be the inner door's open. Or maybe broken. Or just that there's no power to run the lock."

"Is there any other way in?"

"We could try one of the others. Of course, if there's no power . . ."

"Don't need power," Bruce grunted.

"I guess he means there's a manual." Rex searched the smooth metal surrounding the door. "I don't see anything."

Bruce pushed forward and pressed on one of the bolts to the right of the door. The panel came off in his hands, revealing a wheel. "The manual."

Rex stared at him for several moments. "Where on the twenty-three planets did you discover that?"

"Open the door," Bruce answered.

Rex shrugged. "Of course, all this is useless if the inner door is open." Bracing his feet on the corners of the lock cover, he pulled at the wheel.

It began to turn.

After five rotations, it stopped. Quarnian tugged at the door. It opened and the three of them stepped into the lock.

They shut the door behind them. The lock was fairly roomy (another two people could have fit without trouble) and painted faded pale green. A black plastic gauge indicated the lack of air.

"What now?" Quarnian asked. "Will the inner door open?"

"Should," Bruce said. "Doesn't need power."

Rex nodded. "As long as the outer door's sealed, we should be OK." Grabbing another wheel on the inner door, he spun it open.

The air pressure inside suddenly exploded the door open. Quarnian barely missed getting her arm jammed as the door clanged by.

Rex looked at the air gauge on his suit. "There's enough to breathe, all right. We can take off our helmets."

They stuck the collapsible head gear into their pockets as they looked down the corridor in front of them. It was chilly and unlit, a black hole leading to an unknown destination. Rex shined his suitlight down it. The metal of the walls was a combination of colors; the paints had changed like chameleons over the centuries. There was a staleness in the air, as though it had been recycled too many times. Quarnian rubbed a hand along the wall; rough grains of corrosion scratched her palm.

"Doesn't look too lively," Rex commented.

Quarnian nodded. Maybe the crew *had* died out. It would have been difficult to maintain the energy to support them all.

But somehow she didn't think they were all dead.

Something else caught her eye: a series of adhesive pads patched along the wall. They seemed to form a familiar pattern. . . .

Bruce must have seen her look. "Suit hangers," he said.

She nodded. It was easy to comprehend now that she knew what she was looking at: a place for the back, the arms, and the legs of a pressure suit. Only . . .

"Where are the suits now?" she asked.

Rex laughed. "*We* sure can't answer that. Maybe they're just missing from this lock; they could be in others."

It sounded logical, but Quarnian didn't believe it. She looked around; a door handle beside the lock caught her eye. Reaching out, she pulled it open.

It was empty. Perhaps it once had been a storage locker; now it was as bare as Odin's moon.

So where were the suits? Still a mystery. She filed it in her mind; she had a feeling there would be others. "Let's go on."

"Any destination in mind?"

She thought for a moment. "The control room. If there's anyone around, they'll be there."

Rex nodded. "Bruce, which way should we go?"

Bruce pointed to their left.

They went onward, following his finger.

The clang of their feet as they pushed off the walls echoed like sonar through the dark halls. The returning echoes brought no response, however. Occasionally a corridor would branch off from their route, each as dark and haunting as the rest.

They took turns with their suitlights. No telling how long they'd be in there; they'd have to save the batteries.

"How much longer?" Quarnian asked.

He shrugged.

"Seems like we've been here for hours," Rex said.

It wasn't true; her suitwatch showed less than twenty minutes. Still, it seemed much longer. "We don't know where we're going," Quarnian said. "It just seems longer than it is."

"Mmnnn."

They passed another branch.

"Wait a minute," Quarnian said.

Rex looked at her. She could read he was getting tired of this whole business. After the long wait on the *Wreckless*, he had a low tolerance for boredom. He wanted to discover something exciting, but not *too* exciting—he wasn't going to be foolhardy.

She smiled. "I think I can show you something interesting. Look down there."

Rex shined his light. "No different from this one."

"No. Look without the light."

He switched it off. "I don't see . . . Wait a minute."

She nodded. "You see it, too?"

"A glow. Kind of faint. . . . "

"Bruce, what's down that way?"

"Don't know. Quarters, maybe."

"Let's give it a try."

Rex looked skeptical. "We better be careful. We might lose our way."

"We'll find our way back."

"I don't know. . . . "

"Look, we can always leave a trail of breadcrumbs."

Rex smiled, then shrugged. "OK, but just up to the light."

The light glowed softly from a patch on the wall. Quarnian looked at it carefully. It was plastic, with a wavy texture, glowing green with chemical light. She felt puzzled. Chemical lights only lasted a few hours; if this was glowing, someone had been by recently. But there was no sign of life.

The corridor branched off. "Well," she mumbled, "which way now?"

"Back the way we came," Rex answered. "We may never find our way out."

"But someone's been by here."

"They can search for us."

Quarnian began to feel annoyed. Maybe Rex was too cautious. "We're going on," she said firmly. "I just want to know what direction. Bruce, have you any idea?"

"Now, wait a minute," Rex broke in. "Even if there are people here, what makes you think they'll be friendly?"

"We've got beamguns," Quarnian said.

He wouldn't be dismissed by her words. "They'll do us a lot of good in close quarters. And if there's an ambush . . ."

"There's not," Quarnian said, trying to sound sure. She had no idea whether there would be or not; she had an odd lack of feeling about the matter. "Bruce, which way?"

Bruce looked uncomfortable. "Don't know. Been changed."

Before Quarnian could ask what he meant, a light went on to their left. They jumped as the sudden brightness assaulted their eyes.

"I guess the decision has been made for us," Quarnian said. "We go that way."

"Right into an ambush," Rex said as he followed her lead.

The lights led them on like a leash, brightening in front of them and dimming behind. Quarnian began to share Rex's nervousness. Someone knew where they were; they were leading them along for a reason. She hoped it was peaceful.

They floated along, trying to be as silent as they could. The weeks without gravity had made them experts at weightless locomotion. They half flew, half swam, following the brightness.

Finally, after several twists and turns, the light stopped moving.

The section they had arrived in looked just like the rest. A door was set in the wall, its nameplate missing.

"Looks like they want us in there," Rex said.

Quarnian nodded. She knew he wasn't going to open the door. She got them here; it was her responsibility. Besides, if there was danger, she'd probably handle it better than he would; she had more experience with tight spots.

She pushed it open.

The room was dimly lit with a soft glow that contrasted with the harsh glare of the corridors. It was bare. Perhaps it once had been someone's cabin; now only bolts on the walls showed there had been anything but stark metal. It seemed even less used than the corridors; Quarnian had the sudden feeling the door hadn't been open in decades.

A woman floated to Quarnian's left. "Hello," she said, her voice friendly, but with a subtle hint of something wrong. "Welcome to the *Staroamer*."

Chapter Eight

The woman floating in front of Quarnian smiled cheerfully. She seemed to be in her early twenties, with ash-blond hair cut close to her head, and her eyes were a mixture of green and gray. Her skin was pale, as though it were covered with talc, and she wore a thin one-piece jumpsuit, tightly fitting her thin body and colored a conservative gray.

"Who are you?" she asked.

"My name's Quarnian. Quarnian Dow."

"Are you alone?"

Quarnian looked behind her; the two men hadn't followed. Cowards, she thought, smiling to herself. "There are two others," she said quickly, and looked out the door.

Rex and Bruce were waiting for her. "I guess it's safe, huh?" Rex asked, obviously embarrassed.

Quarnian didn't rub it in. "All clear. Come on in."

The two men entered.

"My name's Sindona," the blond woman said.

"Rex Carlssen," Rex said. Quarnian noticed an eagerness in the words.

Bruce grumbled out his own name.

"I tried to meet you near the airlock," Sindona said. "But

51

you had already left. I . . . I decided to lead you here . . . with the lights."

Quarnian weighed the words; there was something wrong with them. "Are you the only one?"

Sindona smiled; something about her expression disturbed Quarnian. "Of course not. There are other . . . others."

"Where are they? The place seems deserted."

"There aren't many of us. Two hundred or so."

"What!" Bruce burst in. "There were over three thousand. . . . " He stopped, as if he was embarrassed to break his habitual silence.

"What happened to everyone?" Quarnian asked.

"Many things. Lack of food. Lack of energy. Radiation that . . . that made nonviable mutations. It's been many years."

Quarnian felt annoyed at the way Sindona kept pausing as she talked. She tried to read her but she was a mix of contradictions. She seemed both open and secretive, trustworthy and deceitful, all at once. "But how—?"

"I'm sure you have many questions," Sindona said. "I'll answer them all, eventually. But I'm being a poor host. Are you hungry?"

"No. I'd like to meet—"

"That's enough, Quarnian," Rex broke in. "We'll find all that out later."

His tone rang alarms in her head. She looked at him. Yes, he was taken in by the pleasant voice and the female form. Rex, the Casanova. Couldn't he see . . . ?

No, he couldn't. He wasn't a syron. He knew only the surface, not the disturbing undertones that were bedeviling her.

And it wasn't so unexpected. She'd been declining his advances for weeks, usually before he even realized he was making them. All that frustration made him ripe for the charms of another female face.

"Well," Quarnian said, feeling a bit more unsure of herself, "when *will* we meet the others?"

Another smile. Quarnian thought she detected a fleeting

hint of fear beneath it. "There's no rush. First we'll get you something to eat. And a place to stay."

"Sounds fine," Rex said. "We can find out everything later."

"Follow me."

Sindona led the way, moving with an economy of effort that made it obvious she was born in weightlessness. Rex, by contrast, had to work hard just to stay with her. Too hard.

Quarnian knew he was planning to make his move on her. The thought disturbed her. She'd have to keep an eye on them both; she had the strongest hunch that Sindona wasn't what she seemed. "Let's go, Bruce," she murmured.

"Don't trust her," the short man said.

Quarnian looked at him for a moment, surprised he had noticed what she had. She nodded and they went after the others.

The meal was a mixture of vegetables in sour-sweet sauce. They ate in silence; Sindona enforced it by shaking her head every time Quarnian began to ask a question. Quarnian had to put her energies into trying to identify the spices involved. It was useless. There were hints of ginger and salt and saffron, but the flavor was none of those, and it left a pleasantly bitter aftertaste. As soon as Sindona seemed ready to speak, she asked what the spices were.

"They . . . they are not Earth spices. We grow them here."

"Grow them? Where?"

"In our gardens. Our diet is monotonous . . . and we have to . . . invent new flavors."

The pauses were driving Quarnian crazy. She wanted to know more than just small talk. "So now tell us. What happened?"

"We're on the edge of our seats," Rex said. "You've been the biggest mystery since the *Marie Celeste*."

"What's that?" Sindona asked.

"Never mind," Quarnian broke in impatiently. "Tell us what happened."

Sindona began, her expression looking as if she realized she couldn't put it off any longer. "Everything went well the first two years. The ship was right on course and on schedule. Then . . . they discovered they were being drawn off course. Captain Zautner tried to correct, but nothing worked.

"There must have been . . . a planet or a protostar near their course. It pulled the ship into its gravity well.

"Of course, the *Staroamer* wasn't designed to fight gravity; it's too big. It took nearly all of our fuel to break away."

She paused as though waiting for a comment; Rex obliged her. "What did they do?"

She smiled and Rex glowed back. "They were off course and they didn't have enough fuel to correct it . . . or to return to Earth. They could only aim for here and . . . hope for luck. I guess we . . . found it."

Quarnian was surprised by the last two words; she thought she could detect a fleeting note of dissatisfaction. But there was something about Sindona that made her damn difficult to read.

"They shut down all nonessentials; they knew they'd be traveling for centuries. Minimum lights, except for in hydroponics. Minimum heat. They decided not to tell Earth what had happened. I assume that's why we're a mystery."

"A big one." Rex smiled. "We were guessing there'd be no one alive, or that everyone would have regressed into barbarians."

Sindona smiled. "The first nearly happened. The first century was . . . the most difficult. People . . ." A frown flickered over her face for an instant. "There was too little food and many died. The population stabilized after that. But we never lost our knowledge of Earth. How could we, with computers that stored the contents of three libraries?"

"Is that how you know so much about us?" Quarnian asked.

"Yes. I . . . I have the position of archivist. That is why they . . . I came to meet you. I know . . . the old language best."

The last sentence came as a surprise to Quarnian. She hadn't considered the possibility that the language would have changed. But she should have, she knew; languages always change over the years. No wonder Sindona was pausing—she had to remember words.

A good explanation. But Quarnian had a feeling it wasn't entirely correct.

Sindona turned to Bruce. "How about you? You haven't said a word since you got here. What questions do you have?"

"None," Bruce mumbled, his face turning red under her attention.

"Bruce knows everything about the ship," Rex said, teasing without malice. "He's our expert."

She looked at him oddly. "Oh, are you?"

"Can we see anyone else now?" Quarnian broke in. She might be able to put her finger on what was wrong with their guide if she had a better frame of reference.

"Not right now. It's . . . late. It's the middle of our sleep period."

"But—"

"We can give you quarters; we've got plenty."

"We're not—"

Once again, Rex jumped in. "We *could* use a rest after all that trooping around here."

Quarnian glared at him, but she could see Sindona was not going to allow further conversation.

And she did feel tired.

"We'll go back to our ship," she mumbled.

"No need for you to go all that way. Follow me."

There were three chambers nearby. "These haven't been used in years," Sindona explained. "We prepared them for you during dinner. Help yourself; I've got to be going." She pushed off and disappeared down the corridor.

Quarnian considered following. No, she felt too tired. She noticed Rex beside her.

"What do you think of her?" Rex asked.

"Don't trust her," Bruce said.

Quarnian nodded her agreement. "There's something fishy around here."

Rex shook his head. "You're too suspicious. I think she's honest." He yawned. "I like her."

For some reason, his words irritated Quarnian. "We'll have to be careful. I have a feeling . . ."

"You've been wrong before. Remember the races." Rex

stretched. "But I don't feel like talking right now. It's been a rough day." He disappeared into one of the cabins.

Quarnian yawned. He was right; she might be wrong. It was hard to tell.

Bruce had chosen his cabin; Quarnian moved into the one remaining. The light switch turned on a pale glow, just enough illumination for her to get her bearings. The room was small, the only respite from bareness an old open-mesh sleepnet and a closet in the corner.

She floated to the side and began to remove her suit; she wasn't about to sleep in it. Besides, it seemed warmer here than in the rest of the ship; they were obviously trying to make their guests at home.

With leaden arms, she removed the last of her suit and pulled herself into the sleepnet. Funny she should be so tired. It wasn't that late for them; the day hadn't been *that* strenuous.

Her eyes felt heavy. There was something wrong here, she thought through the growing fuzz in her brain. I shouldn't be . . .

She realized the food had been drugged just as she drifted off to sleep.

Chapter Nine

Quarnian woke up feeling exceptionally well. She stretched, slowly, bringing her bones into place, ready to take on anything.

It was then she remembered her last thought before dozing off.

She looked at her watch. How long had she been asleep? She had no idea; she hadn't checked since they met Sindona. She might have been out minutes or days.

She reached for the zipper of the sleepnet. Something caught the corner of her eye as she moved.

It was a dot of reddish-brown, hardly bigger than a pinhead, a tiny polka dot against the yellow nylon of the net.

Quarnian looked at her arms. Sure enough, on the left one, just above the elbow, was a tiny speck.

Someone had stuck a needle in her while she was asleep, probably drugging her. But what were they trying to find out?

She noticed a more serious problem when she pulled herself out of the sleepnet: there was no canary yellow in the corner of the room. Her suit was gone, and her beamgun with it.

She tried the door, half expecting it to be locked. It opened easily. Rex was waiting outside.

"Good morning," he said. "If it is morning."

She decided not to mention her discoveries just yet. "You sound cheerful."

"Sure. I just keep thinking about our becoming rich."

"Rich?"

"Sure. I was right about there being a reward for finding this thing. The Earth Heritage Society has put up a lot of money. Ask Bruce if you don't believe me. It was set up ages ago—probably's been collecting interest for five hundred years."

She had forgotten he had mentioned that. "If no other ship follows us here."

"That's not likely. No one would bother coming out so far in this direction. They probably think the *Staroamer*'s a comet or something."

Quarnian wasn't interested. "Oh."

"You don't seem excited. We've gone from rags to riches. When we met, you had nothing."

"I've been rich before." Quarnian felt annoyed at his prattling; there were more important things to worry about.

"Oh? What happened to it? Why'd we have to pawn your necklace?"

Quarnian spit out the answer. "I spent most of it on the revolution on Odin. I had just enough left over to get to New Wichatah."

Rex's eyes registered surprise. "You were involved in that?"

"I asked them to keep it a secret," she replied hastily, not interested in covering the matter further. "It's not important."

"But why didn't you pull your racetrack trick?"

"Let's drop it," she snapped, feeling testy. "There's more to worry about right now."

"Like what?"

"Like the drugs in our food yesterday."

"Drugs? What drugs?"

"Sindona put something in our food. Why do you think we got so tired so fast?"

"It was a long day."

"And what about that needle prick in your arm?"

"What needle?"

Quarnian had his arm in her hands before he was able to finish the sentence. She looked at his elbow.

Nothing.

She checked the other one; the skin was unmarked.

"I think you're letting your hunches get away from you," Rex said, in a mildly mocking manner.

The words irritated her further. "And I suppose it's just my imagination that my spacesuit's missing?"

"So's mine. Sindona probably put them away for safekeeping."

She studied his face carefully. "You're attracted to Sindona, aren't you?"

He didn't even have the decency to look embarrassed. "Yes, I admit it. Don't look so furious. I think it's only natural. I've gone without female companionship since I left New Wichatah."

"Gone without? What am I, a toffil?"

Rex flushed for a moment. "That's not what I mean."

"What do you mean?"

"You know. Stop sounding like a jealous girlfriend."

"I'm not your girlfriend."

"But you *are* jealous. You act like you wish it was you I was after."

"I do not."

Rex didn't answer.

Quarnian decided to drop the subject. It was obvious he had absolutely no idea what she felt. "All right. It's just that I don't trust her."

"You've mentioned that. I think you're wrong."

"You can't see—"

"Hello, everyone," Sindona said.

Quarnian whirled. How much had she heard?

She gave no sign. "Ready for breakfast?"

"Just about," Quarnian mumbled. She would keep an eye on her—and on Rex. It would do no good to confront her now.

"Quarnian seems to think you've stolen our spacesuits."

Sindona smiled. "They've been stored. If you like, you can borrow some of our ... own clothes."

"No, thanks," Quarnian said. She decided she'd need reinforcements. "Is Bruce up? I haven't seen him."

"He is. He's been looking at the ship's archives."

The news surprised Quarnian. She would have thought Bruce was still asleep. Because of his size, any drug would have worn off him more slowly. She couldn't imagine his being given a different dosage. . . .

Rex seemed to have guessed her train of thought; he smiled knowingly.

She ignored it. "What's he looking for?"

Sindona shrugged. "He wanted to ... look around. I assumed that would be the best place to start. I showed him how to work the computer."

"Nice of you."

Sindona ignored Quarnian's sarcasm. "It's my job. I must say, though, that Bruce knows quite a lot about us. More than ... I would have expected."

"The *Staroamer* is a big mystery," Rex said.

"You mentioned that. Would you two like something to eat?"

This time, Quarnian didn't let Rex beat her to it. She was the leader of this expedition; she was going to assert her prerogatives.

But not too roughly; an argument wouldn't help matters. "Yes," she said.

The meal was a form of corn in a tangy sauce; there was no hint of the strange bitterness she had noticed the night before. Perhaps the taste was the drug they had given them—or maybe it was just another part of the flavoring.

After they had finished, Sindona led them to Bruce.

"This is the archive room," she said. "My work place."

The room was as bare as all the others, a hollow space with only a CRT glowing faintly in the murky light. It looked badly worn, its metal dull and pitted with corrosion, its paint chipped and scratched. The numbers on the blue keyboard were barely readable. Letters glowed from the screen, illuminating Bruce's face with a vampire-green light.

"It must have been a great effort to keep all this running," Quarnian commented.

Sindona laughed. "That's an understatement. My generation was lucky. I . . ." Her voice trailed off suddenly.

Quarnian looked at her. "You what?"

"Nothing. It's not important. I just was . . . able to use the power a bit more than my predecessors. We knew . . . we were going to . . . find a star soon."

Every word she spoke made Quarnian believe her story less.

"Of course, we had to cannibalize parts to keep things going. You may have noticed. That's what . . . happened to our scoutships."

"And your spacesuits?" Quarnian asked. "We saw they were missing, too."

Sindona paused for a second; her face twitched. "Yes. The spacesuits, too." She recovered her composure quickly. "I would guess Bruce has seen enough for the time being. What would you like to do?"

"Meet with the captain, for a start," Quarnian said.

"That's being arranged. He's very busy and it may be some time before . . ."

"When?"

"Soon." Sindona suddenly pointed. "I've been meaning to tell you, Quarn. That's quite a nice-looking necklace. A unique design."

Quarnian wasn't fooled by the abrupt change of subject. She decided not to call attention to it. "Yes, it . . ." She stopped. "It's a family heirloom. Oh, I'd prefer it if you didn't call me 'Quarn.' "

Rex smirked; for a second, she thought he was going to tell the truth about the pendant. "I think I'd like to go back to the *Wreckless*."

"The *Wreckless*?"

"Our ship," he explained. "With a 'w.' I think we're going to want a change of clothes." He pulled at his shirt. "This is going to get rancid if we're here any length of time."

Quarnian was about to veto the proposal when she felt a tug on her arm.

Bruce was looking at her. Almost imperceptibly, he nodded.

"Good idea," Quarnian said. "But there's no need for the rest of us to go. Why don't you show him the way, Sindona? Bruce and I will stay here."

"I'm sure we could supply you . . ." Sindona began, looking slightly distressed.

"You heard the boss," Rex said. "Besides, you'll have to get me my suit. Let's go."

Sindona looked resigned. "All right. Follow me. I'll give you a hand." She propelled herself out of the room.

Rex gave Quarnian a disgustingly apparent wink as he left. "We may be awhile. Don't get impatient."

Quarnian felt a hot blaze of annoyance. Thinking with his glands wouldn't help him get to the bottom of this. Still, she guessed that Sindona would have enough principles to resist his advances. She didn't seem the type to jump into bed with a man she just met; she seemed too controlled. Rex was bound to be disappointed.

She turned to Bruce. "Well? What did you want to talk about?"

"Didn't tell us everything."

"You mean you found something?"

"No. Told me how to find what she wanted me to find. Everything's very old—five hundred years ago."

"Anything interesting?"

"All dull. Normal."

"Can you find anything else?"

He shook his head. "Don't know the code."

Quarnian filed the information for future use. "Well, we're probably going to have a long wait. You think you can find your way around the ship?"

"No. Changed. Need map."

She nodded. "Better not to go searching around, then. They've gone to a lot of trouble to keep us in the dark. I wouldn't want to disappear and let them know we're snooping."

Bruce nodded.

"By the way," Quarnian asked, "how *is* it you know so much about the ship? You know a lot more than you should from just seeing a movie."

Bruce looked down at his feet, his face turning pink. "Don't like to talk about myself," he mumbled.

"I know that. Why not?"

He didn't answer, but his face told a story any syron could read. He'd been pushed around all his life, growing up small and ugly in the ugliest part of New Wichatah. Quarnian could see he was intelligent, but knew he never had the chance to show it. She suspected any attempts were curtly and cruelly discounted.

"This isn't New Wichatah," she said softly. "We're partners; I'd like to know."

He looked at her. "You don't talk about *your*self."

Now it was Quarnian who felt embarrassed. "That's different."

Bruce said nothing.

"I'm not ashamed of it or anything," she went on. "There's just so much to tell. Everyone wants to hear it all. I got tired of it years ago."

Bruce regarded her intently. His stare made her feel uncomfortable.

"All right, I'll make a deal," she said. "You tell me what I want to know and I'll answer one question about myself. All right?"

Bruce showed no sign of agreement. Quarnian felt a short flash of temper. Why was she bothering with him at all?

"Promise?" Bruce asked, sounding like a mistrustful child.

She took her pendant in her hand. "I swear by the star."

Bruce nodded. "All right.

"Had a book," he began abruptly, whispering the words as though confessing to a crime. "About the *Staroamer*. Read it over and over. I . . . ." Bruce blushed for an instant at the one-letter word; Quarnian realized it was the first time she had ever heard him use it.

"Go on," she said.

"It told everything about the ship. A copy of the original technical manual." The words were flowing more easily now. "Always knew there were few choices for me. Father—just before he was killed—once said that New Wichatah was too cruel." He touched the scar on his face sadly. "Learned quickly what he meant. Got this at age eight." Bruce's voice had taken on a sad tone, but it quickly picked up in vigor. "Then discovered the book." He smiled. "Practically memorized it. I . . ." He glanced quickly up at her, then, with a growing confidence, repeated the word. "I always wanted to find it."

Quarnian smiled. "A dream come true, then."

He looked at her warily, as though he was trying to see if she was mocking him. "Yes," he said, finally satisfied that she wasn't. "Only it's changed. The design is different. Much different."

"Are you sure you haven't made a mistake?"

He shook his head. "I . . . I haven't forgotten. They have changed the ship."

She shrugged. "I guess we should have expected their tinkering with it all these years. It's probably nothing important."

Bruce shrugged, then spoke. "Your turn, lady."

It took her a moment to remember her promise. "All right," she said, "but just one question."

"What happened to all your money?"

Quarnian felt a chill. "My money? How did you . . . ?"

Bruce's expression gave nothing away.

She smiled. "You probably know as much about me as you do about the *Staroamer*. Well, the answer is simple. I spent it.

Bruce frowned. "Don't joke."

"No joke. Before I came to New Wichatah, I was on Odin."

Once again, Bruce was impressed. "You!"

"I was working with the rebels; they needed the money to overturn the investment bank. It fell, and they were able to use the confusion to remove the Kalif. All I had left was enough to get to New Wichatah. They did promise to repay me when they've rebuilt their economy." She smiled ironically. "Not that I really expect to see it again."

"You spent all that just—"

"The Kalif was insane," Quarnian went on, feeling drained. One explanation always seemed to lead to another. "He had already executed millions. Some rumors said it was for food. It had to be done."

Bruce just stared, wide-eyed.

Quarnian realized she had raised her voice. "Anyway, I knew I had to get to New Wichatah in a hurry. I couldn't even build up funds by gambling: the revolution had disrupted the racing meet. I landed, found Rex, and went to work on getting us here." She waved her hand around the room. "I still can't begin to figure out why. I shouldn't let it bother me, but sometimes I get so . . ."

She stopped. Why was she going on about that?

"I guess I'll have to be more patient," she finished, aware of the lameness of the sentiment.

The door exploded open, hitting the far wall with a bell-like clang. Quarnian turned suddenly to see Rex, his face magenta, huffing and puffing like an angry yellow dragon breathing fire and preparing to lay waste to the countryside.

"What?"

It was as if she had never opened her mouth. "You!" He pointed at Bruce, his hand darting out like a javelin. "You've ruined us!"

Quarnian's temper flared in response to this. She slapped at his hand. "What the frast are you talking about?"

Rex looked at her as though she had just entered the room. "The *Wreckless*," he said, as though the two words explained everything.

"Talk sense," Quarnian said, rapidly losing patience.

"The ship. There's no air in it." He looked her straight in the eye; the twin furies did nothing to cancel each other out. Once again he pointed toward Bruce. "He did it! We're not going to be able to get back to New Wichatah."

Chapter Ten

It seemed to take forever to calm Rex down enough for him to spit out a coherent story. "The ship's airlock was open when I got there. Both doors. The air just blew out. I checked the inner door; it hadn't been closed properly." He looked at Bruce with an aura of menace.

"Wait a second," Quarnian broke in. "I thought there were interlocks. How were we able to open the outer door?"

Rex lost a bit of steam. "They were broken. I didn't have time to get them fixed before we left." He returned to his bluster, but there was a lessening of force. "But that doesn't matter. If the door had been properly closed . . ."

"Why do you think Bruce did it?" Quarnian asked calmly.

"He was the one who—"

"Oh, frast. You were the one—"

"I remember distinctly—"

"You have no idea. It was yesterday. Do you seriously believe you can remember something as unimportant as that?"

"Unimportant? It was . . ."

But there was something missing from his anger. Quarnian knew she had hit a nerve. "Anyway, I was the one who left the outer door open. Why don't you blame me for it?"

Rex didn't answer.

"Well?"

"It couldn't be you," he mumbled.

"Why? Because you like me and mistrust Bruce?"

"I don't like you," Rex murmured.

Quarnian found the words surprisingly painful. A sudden tightness clutched her chest, but the feeling passed quickly. "It may not have been any of us."

"Then, who—"

"Someone from the *Staroamer*."

Rex looked at her as though she had suggested he give up sex. "Are you crazy? Sindona stayed inside. She couldn't—"

"I'm not talking about her, necessarily. It could have been any of them."

"But why?"

Quarnian shrugged. "It may have been an accident." She didn't think so. With the crystal clarity of a sure thing, Quarnian knew it had been deliberate.

Rex shook his head slowly. "They couldn't. They don't have any spacesuits."

"How do you—"

"We didn't see any."

"So what? There must be some somewhere. What if they had to make repairs to the hull?"

She could tell Rex knew he was beaten. "I still don't think they did it," he grumbled, a fighting action to cover his retreat.

She knew better than to press. "It doesn't make any difference, anyway. We've got to live with the situation. Is there any way of filling it up again?"

Rex shook his head. "We're not flush with the airlock; we'd have to bring everything in with tanks."

"Can we stay in suits?" Bruce broke in quietly, as though he was now sure the shouting was over.

"All the way to New Wichatah? Or maybe Gemma?" Rex laughed.

"Aren't we moving nearer to them?" Quarnian asked quickly.

"Sure. We'll get maybe two weeks out. Our suits have air for six hours."

"We'll manage," Quarnian said. "There's probably some other way."

"Another one of your hunches?" Rex sneered.

Quarnian didn't reply; the issue was never going to be resolved. What command she had of this expedition was rapidly slipping through her fingers.

"Where's Sindona?" Bruce asked.

The two looked at him as though he were speaking another language.

"Sindona," he repeated.

Quarnian turned to Rex. "Well?"

"She was right behind me. . . . "

"She's not here now," Quarnian said quietly.

"Well, *I* don't know. Maybe she went for help."

"Do you really think so?"

Rex couldn't meet her eyes. "No," he said, very softly.

"Don't trust her," Bruce said.

Rex glared. "There's nothing wrong with Sindona. There's probably a good explanation."

Quarnian could see Bruce starting to smirk; she knew she had to head it off. "You're probably right, Rex. I don't trust her, but I think she's basically a good sort, if that makes any sense." She smiled. "Another one of my hunches."

Rex smiled back; she was happy to see it. "I'll let you have that one."

"Right. Now we'll have to think of a plan of action."

"Search the ship," Bruce grunted. "Find the crew. They're hiding."

Quarnian nodded. "I think—"

"Hello, everyone."

They all turned to face Sindona. She smiled at them, unbothered by the looks on their faces. "Sorry . . . I had to leave you."

"Where were you?" Quarnian asked.

"I was talking to the captain. I . . . I wanted to know . . . if there was anything we . . . could do."

"Is there?"

She shook her head. "We have nothing to . . . spare right now. But there shouldn't be a problem. We'll contact the planet when we get nearer; there'll be others here to visit."

Rex looked at Quarnian as though he thought Sindona's words proved something. Quarnian ignored him. "You talked with the captain. Can we?"

"He's very busy. . . . "

"He had time to talk with you."

"But . . ." Her pause was a long one this time; her eyes seemed to lose focus for a moment. "I guess there won't be any problem. Come with me. Just Quarnian."

Quarnian was surprised by the sudden turnabout. Pushing off quickly, she went to follow.

The corridors slowly became darker and dingier; fewer and fewer lights were working. At least the captain's no autocrat, Quarnian thought. His living quarters looked worse than where she had been.

She tried to keep track of the twists and turns; she didn't want to have to depend on a guide all the time. She found it difficult; with no reference points, one twist looked just like another.

"Is this the way to the control room?"

"No," Sindona said. "The captain's . . . in his quarters right now. You can see the bridge some other time."

Quarnian knew her tone meant "never."

Finally, after passing a light that flickered like a too-slow strobe, Sindona took her into another cabin to meet the second member of the crew to consent to show himself: the captain.

Her first thought was that they hadn't chosen their leader on looks. The captain was short and chubby, with scruffy white hair and a wispy beard. His pallor was more pasty than Sindona's whiteness; he reminded Quarnian of a grub. The skin had an oily sheen to it. He wore a jumpsuit similar to Sindona's; the only alterations were those made necessary by his size.

"Hello," the man said. "I'm Captain Vorst."

There was something strange about the way he said it.

The words came out mechanically, as though he had read them in books but wasn't used to speaking them. "I'm Quarnian Dow. We're here to—"

"Sindona told me why you're here. I'm sorry I wasn't ... able to see you before now. I've been ... occupied."

Quarnian noticed his eyes dart between Sindona and her as he spoke. "We haven't seen any of your crew, either."

"They are very busy." He paused for a moment, his eyes turning to Sindona again. "There are so few of us to do so much."

His voice was sounding more natural now. "We've also had a problem with our ship," Quarnian said.

"Sindona told me that, too. I am sorry."

"Can't you help?"

"Excuse me, Captain," Sindona interrupted. "I must go out for a few minutes."

A puzzled expression crossed his face for an instant before he nodded and Sindona left.

"Can't you help?" Quarnian repeated, ignoring the unpleasant feeling her guide's departure had left her.

"No," Vorst said. "We don't have the ... We can't ..."

Quarnian watched him search for the words.

"No air for you," he concluded. "We cannot ... spare any."

He suddenly looked very nervous. She tried to read him, but could pick up nothing definite, only the hunch he was somehow dangerous. She couldn't see why.

"But you'll be going by New Wichatah in a few weeks. You'll be able to land there."

"Can't land."

Quarnian remembered what Sindona had said about the ship being too big. "Well, you can ..."

Sindona returned abruptly. "Sorry. I've been drinking too many liquids lately. What were you talking about?"

Vorst's nervousness was gone. "I was telling Quarnian we couldn't spare any air." He turned to Quarnian, sure of himself now. She wondered how Sindona's presence made any difference. "We aren't able to land on any planet."

"Then you can ferry down," Quarnian said. "The point is, you won't have to conserve anymore. The trip is over."

"Not for us," Sindona said. "We ... we've been weightless all our lives. We just can't go down into gravity."

Quarnian reddened; she should have realized they'd need time to adjust. "But still, once you orbit, there'll be help, so if you gave us some air ..."

"All you say is true," the captain said. "But it applies to you, too. Why can't you just wait until we make contact with your planet?"

"Because ..." Because she had a feeling they'd be better off away from the *Staroamer*? Because she felt they had deliberately trapped her inside? She couldn't say that. "Because I feel very cooped up in here."

Vorst laughed, each "ha" enunciated separately. "You'll get used to it. Meanwhile, you are our guests. Sindona, show them around the ship. I've got work to do."

Sindona nodded. "This way."

Quarnian pushed off behind her. She had other questions, but she knew the answers wouldn't satisfy her.

"This way," Sindona said as they entered the corridor, taking the fork to the left.

"Didn't we come from the other direction?"

"What? No. You just got turned around, that's all."

Quarnian stared at the twin corridors. Sindona was lying; Quarnian noticed the light strobing in the right fork. Should she mention that? No. There was no reason for confrontation just yet; it seemed safer to keep storing data, preparing for the right moment.

"Come on," Sindona said, taking Quarnian's hand.

Quarnian felt more than just flesh. A stiff wad of paper touched her palm.

She followed Sindona, wondering what was up.

When Sindona's hand left, the paper remained. Quarnian began to bring her hand up to read it.

Sindona stopped the motion with a hand on her wrist. "Later," she said, forcing her meaning into the word. "I'll show you the rest of the ship."

Quarnian got the message. She followed quietly, the paper burning questions into her head.

They turned through the maze. Nothing was familiar until they suddenly stopped.

"This is your cabin," Sindona said. "Wait here; I'll get the others."

As soon as she disappeared, Quarnian looked at the paper. Five words were printed on it in a hurried scrawl.

"I am on your side," it said.

Quarnian didn't pay attention to Sindona's grand tour. It was unenlightening; doors were (unfortunately) locked, members of the crew were hidden away. Even though it took the whole afternoon, Quarnian knew there'd be nothing important to see.

Besides, she had too much on her mind to care where they went.

What did the note mean? Was Sindona trying to help them off *Staroamer*? Or was it just a trick to make them trust her?

And why the note in the first place? Sindona had had plenty of opportunity to talk with her.

Worst of all, Quarnian didn't even have a hunch about what to do about it.

She was startled out of her thoughts by Bruce's voice. "Nothing's like it should be," he muttered close to her ear.

She nodded, wondering if she should tell him about the note. But she knew what he would vote for: a trick.

"Leading us around in circles, too."

"What?" she whispered.

"Do you have a question?" Sindona asked.

"No," Quarnian said, feeling as if she had gotten caught whispering in school. "No, nothing."

"All right, I guess that's about it. I suppose you're hungry by now."

Quarnian looked at her face; she wanted her to say yes. "Sure," she said. "How about you Rex?"

Rex mumbled something; he'd been even less communicative than Bruce since he discovered the trouble with the *Wreckless*. She took it for an assent.

They were only a short distance from where they had eaten before; Quarnian knew it had been planned that way. Dinner was waiting for them, vegetables served without sauce. In some ways, the taste of peas and carrots was reassuring. Quarnian reached out for a drinking bulb to wash it down.

"Here," Sindona said. "Let me help you with that."

Quarnian caught a tenseness in her voice; it stopped her from protesting when Sindona grabbed the bulb. "There," the blond woman said, tapping the side of the bulb with her thumb.

Right where the nail ended, the word "no" was scratched.

Quarnian looked at Sindona again; her expression convinced her not to ask any questions. She remembered the drug in the first meal and pretended to take a sip.

Sure enough, a half hour after they ate, Rex and Bruce were talking about turning in early.

Quarnian went along with the gag. She slipped into her sleepnet and waited.

Chapter Eleven

Quarnian must have dozed; a touch on her shoulder snapped her awake.

"Quarnian?" whispered a shadow in the dark.

"Sindona?" Quarnian reached for the light; she thought she had left it on.

A hand grabbed hers. "No, don't. They might notice the use of power."

"They?"

"The rest of the crew. They keep an eye on those things."

Reluctantly, Quarnian saw her point. She wished she could see Sindona's face, though; it was the best way for her to tell if she was telling the truth.

"I suppose you have a lot of questions."

"Does a star burn hydrogen? I want to know what's going on here. What have you been keeping from us?"

Quarnian seemed to sense Sindona was smiling. "I knew you'd wonder about the history program; that's why I let you look at it while I went with Rex. The captain was sure you wouldn't notice, but I know a lot more about human curiosity than he does."

"Human curiosity? You mean he's not human?"

Sindona sighed. "You don't miss a thing. You don't know how dangerous it is for me to speak to you like this. But I need your help and I know I won't get it unless I tell you what's going on. I'll just have to risk it."

"Is the captain human?" Quarnian asked again.

"It's not easy to explain. I've been running it through my head since I first met you." Sindona paused. "All right, let's start this way. Humans descended from apes, right? But something had to spark that change. One day, for some reason, an ape decided to leave the trees and live on the plains. All human evolution stems from that decision." She faltered a moment. "At least, that's what the tapes say. I'm not quite sure what plains are, but that's what they say."

Quarnian picked up a sadness in the last words; Sindona had sounded like an old shuttlebum she had once met on the Borna run who longed to pilot again.

Once again, Sindona's voice broke through the darkness. "People had been living on the plains—on planets—for millions of years. When they went into space, they searched out similar environments, or brought Earth with them. 'Evolution is a game for explorers.' I remember that from one of the old booktapes. We were explorers. We evolved."

"That's crazy. Evolution takes centuries—millions of years."

"On Earth. But there's more radiation out here; it moves faster. Plus, we made a few genetic improvements ourselves."

Quarnian saw there was no use debating the point; obviously something had happened here that they were trying to hide from her. Maybe this was the answer—or maybe it was just a fantastic story to eliminate her suspicions. "Go on."

"After the accident, the *Staroamer* became a different environment. Certain traits became important for man for the first time since the apes left the trees."

"Like what?"

"Well, we had to conserve energy. No lights. So, naturally, those with better night vision had a slight advantage. Some of us can now see infrared, although most of the crew just have an extreme sensitivity to visible light."

"Which is why they stay away from us?"

"Some of them. The light you need would be too much."

"What else?"

"Well, the biggest change . . ." Sindona paused. "No, you won't believe me if I just tell you flat out." She thought for a moment. "We'll try it this way. What would be the biggest danger when you live your life in a spaceship?"

Quarnian shrugged. "I don't know."

"Guess."

"Well . . . I suppose the most dangerous situation would be loss of pressurization. But I don't think that should . . ." She stopped; her intuition was humming. "No," she whispered. "You can't mean that."

"Exactly. Sections depressurize every once in a while. Some people can survive just a little bit longer than others in vacuum. It becomes an important survival trait. And over the years . . ."

"You can live in vacuum! That's why you don't have spacesuits!"

"Exactly. They call themselves spacebreathers—although the name's more poetic than accurate."

"But how—"

"Basically, they hold their breath. Their pulse slows down, their blood only goes where it's most needed, and the oxygen in their lungs—which have become oversized—lasts a long time. It's like seals or dolphins on Earth. The only difference is that they're in water and we're in vacuum."

"That's a big difference," Quarnian muttered.

"The best of them can stay outside for almost an hour."

Quarnian felt a tight feeling in the depth of her stomach. What type of creatures had she been stuck with? "What else?" she asked wearily.

"Well, there's mindspeaking—not mind reading; we can just project thoughts to one another. Lower nutritional requirements. Joints slightly different. They're a different race. Almost a different species altogether."

"Almost?"

"Not quite, of course. They're still interfertile with humans. That's why you're being kept here."

Quarnian shivered; it had nothing to do with the temperature. "What do you mean?" she asked despite the feeling she knew what the answer would be.

"They tested you and Rex last night. They like your genes. Yours especially. They need new ones; genetic manipulation can only do so much. They're not going to let you leave here."

Quarnian remembered the needle scab on her arm. "They tested Rex, too? I didn't see any sign of it on him."

"They just did a better job. You must have moved while they did it. They didn't bother with Bruce. Too much of a throwback."

"But why us? They'll be nearing New Wichatah soon; there are bound to be people who might want to join them."

"They're not going anywhere near there."

"What?"

"They want to keep on going. They'll pick up some power from a local sun and head off into space."

"But why?"

Sindona sighed. "They want to see how far they can evolve."

Quarnian didn't have a reply. The fantastic story had the ring of reality. And yet . . . she wished she could see Sindona's face. "Why are you telling me this?" she whispered.

"I like you. You're different from your friends—you're very much like me. Besides, I knew I'd need your help."

Quarnian shook her head. "That's not what I mean. These are your people. Why are you betraying their plans?"

A profound sadness took root in Sindona's voice. "They're not my people. I feel like . . . like the Neanderthals must have felt when the next step came along. I'm an atavism; I'm out of place here. I want to escape; I've always wanted to, right from the moment I learned we'd be near a planet in my lifetime. And I need your help to do it."

As far as Quarnian could make out, the emotion seemed genuine. She nodded. "I understand. But I might not be able to do anything."

"Don't say that. We can take charge of this escape."

Quarnian suppressed a sigh. She didn't want to mention

that the crew seemed to be pulling the strings this time. And
yet . . .

There had to be some reason why her intuition led her
here. Maybe it *was* to rescue Sindona. "What do you want
to do?"

"I don't know yet. I'll have to find a way to get some air in
your ship. Once we leave, they won't change course to chase
us." She seemed to be suppressing a rising excitement. "We
can escape."

Quarnian nodded. She didn't like the idea of being an
evolutionary guinea pig, a baby machine, producing a new
generation of near-aliens. "We'll manage somehow," she
murmured, not really believing it. All her feelings were
intensely pessimistic—and she didn't dare to search for a
hunch. She was too afraid of what it might be.

"I'd better go now," Sindona said. "Don't let anyone
know what I've told you; pretend this never happened. You
see, you . . ." She paused for an instant. "I'll explain later.
Just be very careful."

Quarnian heard her scrambling away. "Wait a minute,"
she called as a thought exploded in her head like a delayed
bomb. "You said I was like you. What did you . . . ?"

The latching of the door was the answer to her question.

Quarnian tried to sort out her thoughts; she couldn't.
There was too much information to digest; it quickly
became a blur as it crowded together in her mind.

But one thought dominated: was Sindona telling the
truth?

She tried to stretch her intuition; nothing came to mind.
One of the drawbacks: you couldn't depend on it when you
needed it.

There were too many unanswered questions and Quarnian was too tired. She closed her eyes and tried to rest,
praying she'd be able to fall asleep. She had a feeling her
prayer wouldn't be answered.

The earliest time she thought it seemly, Quarnian
dragged herself to the archive room. She felt detached, her
mind awake but her body half asleep. It was hard for her to
focus her eyes on the ancient CRT. The little green numbers

and letters seemed to dance in front of her. She wondered if there was any chance of finding some coffee.

The keys took all her attention as she punched in her questions. Too often, the answer was DATA NOT AVAILABLE. Infuriatingly noncommittal.

She began feeling a bit more awake; the numbers steadied and the heaviness in her eyelids lessened. She began to work harder, trying to find information, anything that might back up Sindona's story. She needed proof; her current half belief wasn't nearly enough.

She was concentrating so hard she lost track of everything.

"Lady?" came a voice closely behind her.

Quarnian jumped, ready to do battle with the intruder. She had almost done something rash when she recognized Bruce.

He tried to back away, but he had no purchase. He floated gently in zero gee.

"I'm sorry, Bruce. You startled me. What time is it?"

"Eleven hundred, ship time." He grunted the words grudgingly, hiding behind monosyllables.

She shook her head. "I didn't realize it was so late. What's our tour director have planned today?"

"Tour director?"

"Sindona."

"Don't know." Bruce's voice was filled with foreboding.

"What's the matter?"

"Just woke up. Drugged."

"Drugged?" Quarnian asked with as much surprise as she could muster; she was glad Bruce wasn't a syron. "Like the first night?"

Bruce was puzzled. "Just last night. Once was mickeyed. Know the feeling."

Quarnian suddenly remembered what Sindona had said about not testing Bruce. It was a partial confirmation, anyway. She nodded noncommittally.

"Sindona's up to something. Should do something."

"Do something? What?"

There was a hint of repressed violence in Bruce's expression. "On New Wichatah you learn how to get the truth."

The threat in his tone chilled her. "That's not necessary. You see . . ." Quarnian remembered Sindona's warning. She doubted Bruce would spill anything, and yet . . .

She'd better wait until she knew the situation.

"See what?"

"I'm on top of things, Bruce. I'll make sure she doesn't—"

The door to the room opened, clanging against the metal of the bulkhead. Rex entered, looking falsely nonchalant, but even a child could see he was upset about something. "Have you seen Sindona?" he asked, a tightness in his voice showing his concern.

Bruce shook his head.

"No," Quarnian said. "Why?"

"She's missing."

"Missing?" The word gave her a chill. "What do you mean?"

"Just what I said. I've been looking for half an hour. She's not in her cabin."

Quarnian wondered why he was near her cabin. The answer returned immediately. "Did you look inside, just to make sure," she asked, her voice filled with sarcasm so intense it surprised her.

A redness bloomed in Rex's cheeks.

"Maybe she didn't want to bed down with you."

Rex stared at her for a moment. "All right, I admit I had that in mind. But she's still not there, no matter what my motive was. I'm worried."

"Why are you so . . ." Quarnian stopped. Rex had every right to make passes at Sindona. There was no reason to be bitter about it; she had no cause to act so jealous. "I'm sorry," she said. "I'm sure she'll turn up. After all, where could she go?"

Rex smiled, but Quarnian was bothered by her own words. Had the crew members found out what she had told her? They had put a lot of effort into keeping their visitors in the dark; the one who showed them some light might be in danger.

"I suppose we really should go after her," Quarnian said.

"I don't want to be stuck around here all day. If we spread out and . . ."

Bruce shook his head vigorously. "Stay together. May be trouble."

Rex laughed. "Trouble? What makes you think so?"

Bruce shrugged. "Hunch."

Rex laughed long and loudly. "Now you're doing it, too. At least Quarnian has an excuse."

Quarnian could see Bruce bristle at the scorn in Rex's words; he looked ready to begin a fight. "Bruce, please leave us alone for a few minutes."

"Why? I can tell that little runt anything I—" Rex continued.

"Bruce, leave the room."

Her voice allowed no argument; Bruce stepped outside after a threatening glance at Rex.

"Why are you bothering to—?"

"Rex, stop it. If we're going to get out of here, we're going to have to work together."

"Why? We'll be down in New Wichatah in a few weeks. Rich, too, if we're able to convince the Earth Heritage Society. . . .

"OK, Rex." Quarnian resisted the urge to tell him Sindona's tale. "You didn't feel that way when you found out about the air yesterday."

Rex shrugged. "Well, frast, I might as well make the best . . ." The smile on his face faded as he caught Quarnian's expression. "I mean . . ."

"How do you feel about Sindona?" Quarnian asked.

"She's very attractive, I'll admit that. And it's been a long time since . . . Well, she's very attractive."

"Do you love her?"

"What kind of question is that?"

"One you haven't answered."

Rex said nothing for a few moments. "I don't—and I don't plan to. I'd go crazy if I let myself fall for every woman I took a liking to."

"Is that what women are to you?"

"No, of course not." Rex was red. "If the right one came along, I know I'd want more than just sex. I have feelings, too. But I'm not planning anything permanent—just a little bit of fun while we're stuck here."

Quarnian wished he weren't even planning that. Still, the words were something of a relief. "All right, do whatever you want with her—with her consent, of course."

Rex bristled. "I'm no—"

"You're right. You're not." Quarnian rubbed her face slowly. "I'm sorry, Rex. I'm a bit cross. I didn't sleep too well last night and I don't know what I'm saying. I'm too tired."

"So what are we going to do about finding Sindona?"

Quarnian stifled a yawn, partly as a show, partly because it was the way she felt. "Let's wait. She may be with the captain or something. I need a nap right now. If she doesn't show up by the time I wake, we'll go after her."

Rex nodded and Quarnian turned to leave.

"Oh, and Rex," she said as she was about to pass through the door.

"Yes?"

"Please be sure to lay off Bruce. We're a team and we've got to stick together."

"I didn't choose that little runt to—"

"Please, Rex. For me. I've got too much on my mind to have to keep you two from each other's throats."

She had picked the right tone; Rex's resolve melted. "Well . . . for you."

"Thank you, Rex," Quarnian whispered. She took off for her cabin and a dreamless nap.

Chapter Twelve

Quarnian woke up suddenly; someone was in her cabin again. "Sin–" she began.

She found herself unable to finish.

Her muscles had turned rigid; she began to shake in a gentle but uncontrollable vibration that terrified her.

Four hands unzipped her sleepnet and she felt herself being pulled roughly out of the room.

She tried to get a look at her captors but her eyes only twitched, moving at random like the rest of her body. She could only guess that they were crew members.

The tics and shivers increased.

What had they done to her? She tried to gain control over her random movement, but everything she attempted only made things worse.

"Do not . . . move," said a voice behind one of her ears. "It will be easier."

She gave up trying. If Sindona had been telling the truth, they wouldn't do anything to hurt her so as not to risk losing her precious genes.

As she was pushed expertly along the ship's corridors, she

tried not to panic. She had been in worse troubles than this. That time on Radis . . .

She felt herself being tossed aside, into a cabin that branched off the corridor. All she saw was muddy green; she heard the sound of a door being closed.

Then, as abruptly as it had been lost, she regained control of herself again.

She pushed off for the door: locked. There was a hole the size of her fist cut into it about a meter and a half from the deck.

Quarnian looked through it but all she saw was the wall of the corridor.

"All right," she said to herself. "Why are they doing this?"

She found it suddenly easier to think. She had been locked up before; she could take it. But that awful feeling that she had no control over her own body . . .

Quarnian shuddered. Some weapon. But what was it? A paralyzer was just a mad scientist's dream. How were they able to come up with one?

She wasn't sure if she wanted to know the answer. If the crew had something like that, what other things might they have up the sleeves of their jumpsuits?

Quarnian decided she was asking herself too many questions.

She explored the rest of her cell, but there was little to see. It was cold and bare, without even a sleepnet. Like the rest of the *Staroamer,* it had an unused, musty aroma, but somehow here it seemed far worse.

"The Black Hold of the *Calcutta,*" she said, shaking her head. "I've got to get out of here."

Breaking through the door was out of the question; she found that out quickly enough. It was in perfect repair.

Maybe when they brought her food . . . No, they'd just paralyze her again. The gun or whatever it was probably fit through the hole in the door.

But there had to be a way . . .

She suddenly got the distinct impression someone was watching her.

She looked out the door: no one. But who . . . ?

"Quarnian!" a voice hissed.

Quarnian turned, expecting to see someone suddenly materialized behind her. The cell was still empty.

"Over here. By the corner."

It took a short search to find the source, a small hole rusted through the wall near the place where two walls joined. Quarnian floated closer and put her eye to it.

She saw only the dim outline of another eye. "Who's that?" she asked.

"Sindona."

"You!" Quarnian felt her anger rising. "I guess you're satisfied now. I was an idiot to—"

"Satisfied? What? Oh, you think I put you here."

"It's an obvious conclusion."

"No, I didn't. I'm in a cell myself."

"What?" Somehow Quarnian believed her. "Why?"

"They found out what I told you. They thought you'd be better off in here, too—at least until it's too late for you to leave."

"That's crazy. Bruce and Rex'll start wondering where I am."

"I know. But the crew doesn't understand that. People disappear all the time on ship; they're reassigned or they just want to go off to another section. No one thinks about it."

"I'll tell Vorst."

"I doubt he'd listen."

Quarnian cursed. "Damn it, how'd you let it all slip? After all that time you spent warning me not to say anything—"

"They didn't learn it from me."

"Then how?"

"From you."

"Me? I never said . . ." And Sindona's words of the previous night returned to her. What had she called it? Mindspeaking. Projecting their thoughts. And if you can project thoughts, you certainly can receive them. Evidently they were different from the telepaths that had been discovered on Earth, the ones who could only communicate with another who had the same talent.

"They can read anyone's mind?" Quarnian asked, feeling herself falling into a crevasse of depression.

"No, they can't," Sindona said. "Only those who are sensitive."

"But I'm n–" The words died on her lips. Was that what made her a gold star? Did a little telepathy go a long way toward making a syron?

"What's a syron?"

Quarnian felt sick. "Tell me about this mindspeaking. Does everyone here do it?"

"Just about. I was about to warn you when I had to leave. They were looking for me; I just had to hope you wouldn't project. I should have known it wouldn't work; you're a very strong projector. But what's a syron?"

Reluctantly, Quarnian told her everything.

"You can see the future?" Sindona asked when she was through. "Do you see if we can get away from the *Staroamer*?"

"I can't," Quarnian said. They never understood.

"What question are you answering?"

Despite herself, Quarnian smiled. "Both."

"Do you have any feelings about it at all?"

Quarnian tried to think, to get in touch with her instincts. She had been afraid to consider their chances, afraid of what she might see. But she couldn't put it off forever. Now was as good a time as ever. She let her mind go and waited for her intuition to bring back an answer.

And it came. "I think," Quarnian said slowly, fighting despair. "I think we're not going to get out of here."

The spoken words solidified her hunch.

Sindona was quiet for several moments. "If that's true," she finally asked, "why did you come here in the first place?"

"I don't know!" Quarnian fought to keep the fear out of her voice. "I just came. I never know . . ."

There was a short silence. "All right," Sindona said just about the time Quarnian felt ready to apologize, "maybe you're wrong. That's happened before, hasn't it?"

"Sometimes."

"All right, then. We may still get out of this."

"We?"

"You don't miss a thing." Quarnian could hear Sindona's smile. "I'm going to be leaving with you."

"Now, here's my plan. . . . " Quarnian said.

"What?"

"Forget it. It's a joke. Look, we're not exactly free to do anything."

"They'll let us out; I'll tell the captain you're willing to make a deal. Then we can work on getting air into your ship."

Quarnian sighed. "You forget why I'm in here in the first place. I'll just give everything away."

"We'll work on that, too. You can learn to control what you're projecting, just like the rest of us."

Quarnian shook her head. "It's no good. It looks so hopeless."

"You give up too easily. We have to make our own chances."

"But we have none. Don't you understand? We're stuck here. It's inevitable."

"Nothing is inevitable."

Quarnian didn't answer; she didn't want a philosophical debate right now. But she knew better than Sindona; everything is inevitable. Everything in the universe was plotted out; you only thought otherwise because you never saw the pages. Sindona would soon discover that.

"Quarnian?"

"Sorry. I was thinking." Well, maybe her intuition was wrong. She'd been on a good streak lately; maybe it had come to an end.

"You've got to start working."

Quarnian nodded. "On controlling my thoughts. What do I do?"

"I don't know. Give me a minute." There was a scuffling on the other side of the partition as Sindona moved. "I guess the first thing will be to teach you how to receive. Let's see now . . . this is going to be difficult—sort of like explaining to someone how to see. It's just so natural for us. . . . "

"Wonderful. You're really building up my confidence."

"Shh. Just concentrate. Listen, but not with your ears. With your mind."

Quarnian concentrated. She had no idea what to expect. Would she hear a voice in her head? Would the words suddenly appear in her brain, big glowing letters she could read like a book. Or was it . . . ?

"Stop worrying. Just relax."

Well, at least she had confirmation that she was projecting. She couldn't be doing it all the time; otherwise she never would have had to explain anything to Sindona. A tiny consolation. She tried to concentrate on nothingness.

It was impossible. Thoughts kept intruding. Dark thoughts of failure and imprisonment.

"Please, Quarnian. Relax."

She relaxed; maybe she could go back to her interrupted nap. *You're giving up too easily*, she told herself. *We can find a way out. I can help you with the layout of the* Staroamer *and then we can figure out some way to get air into the* Wreckless. *I'll tell the captain that—*

Quarnian felt her heart hiccup. "Sindona! I—I think . . ."

"You read me loud and clear. Or is the term loudly and clearly? I have trouble remembering those old idioms."

"But . . . it was like—like I thought the thought myself." Quarnian felt a shiver. How could she tell her own thoughts from those of others?

You can tell, she—no, Sindona *thought*.

Quarnian still felt doubtful. It was a creepy feeling to have to wonder whether your thoughts were really someone else's.

We'll work on that, Quarnian. It'll just take some time.
Yes, I suppose it will.

"Very good. We're making progress." Sindona's voice startled her. *We'll keep you from talking in no time.*

Quarnian grinned. She could almost drink the happy excitement in Sindona's thoughts. Maybe it was what she had been doing all along; reading the emotions of others to arrive at her hunches. Maybe she'd be better able to differentiate between her thoughts and Sindona's, given time and practice. "What next, professor?"

"I'll have to—"

The voice cut off abruptly.

"Sindona?" Quarnian whispered, startled and frightened by the sudden silence. "What . . . ?"

The door to Quarnian's cell clanged open. A crewman stood in the doorway, small, piggy eyes focusing on her warily. His hair had just a faint tinge of red in the whiteness, like drops of blood mixed with snow. "Come with me," he said, his thick, fleshy lips pronouncing the words in a voice rusty with disuse.

"Where are we going?"

"To see the captain," the man grunted.

Quarnian was surprised to see Sindona waiting with the captain, but she realized he needed her to coach him how to pronounce words.

Quarnian started. Did she think that or had Sindona? She shook her head. It didn't matter, she supposed, but this mindspeaking was going to have to take some getting used to.

"Your . . . friends are asking about you," Vorst said. "The small one has . . . threatened violence. We cannot allow that."

"What do you want me to do about it?" Quarnian snapped.

"Tell them not to attempt escape. We don't want to hurt you or . . . Rex."

"What about Bruce?"

"We're not interested in him. If he makes too much trouble, we'll have to eliminate him."

"Listen, you bloated—"

Sindona jumped in. "Don't speak that way. Be polite to our great leader."

The captain didn't seem to notice the sarcasm. "Sindona is right. We will be together from now on."

Quarnian was about to tell him what she thought about the whole idea, but Vorst spoke first. "Those angry thoughts will change nothing. You are part of the crew now."

The words puzzled Quarnian until she realized she had been projecting again. Was there any way to stop herself?

Vorst grinned as though he knew he had a secret weapon.

She knew her job would be even more difficult than she had imagined. "Can I tell Rex and Bruce the truth?"

Vorst shrugged. "If they don't try to leave, that will be satisfactory. We only want your genes."

Quarnian didn't like the way he said it. She doubted the ship had facilities for an artificial womb. The human body was a much more efficient way to make more human bodies, anyway. But she had no desire to become a baby machine. Worse—she knew she'd have little choice as to who would be the father.

Maybe he would listen to reason. "Why us?" she asked, not really believing it would do any good. "All you have to do is to land on New Wichatah and you'll have all the genes you need."

"We cannot."

"Well, orbit, then."

"No. You . . . misunderstand. We cannot. The inhabitants are . . . primitive."

"We're advanced enough for you."

"Genetically, yes. But socially . . . I am not sure. You know by now we are an advance on the human race. They would be jealous of our difference."

"Not really. . . ."

"We are too strange for them; we have strengths that they have not. People fear others' strengths." Vorst grinned like a fat death's-head. "I have seen some of the tapes, have I not, Sindona?"

Sindona nodded.

Quarnian didn't give up. "Just because you can do things people can't doesn't mean they're . . ." The thought became paralyzed in her mouth. How did people feel about syrons? "Well, there's always trade. I'm sure you can use—"

"We cannot interrupt the . . . journey," the captain said, a final cap to his argument.

Quarnian recognized the tone; she knew better than to pursue the subject. It was the tone of a zealot. She had seen the same type of thinking before. The captain's mind traveled in familiar ruts. No amount of logic and common sense would break him away from what he had been taught since childhood. You need leverage for that, some threat that

could make him able to challenge the axioms of his life. Her
voice wasn't going to be enough.

She returned to Vorst's last words. "Your journey?
Where?"

"To the future." Vorst smiled again; Quarnian was beginning to hate the sight of his incisors. "We are the beginning
of a new race. One day, we'll be ready to meet humans
again. Then we'll return."

"To conquer."

Vorst looked shocked. "No. To help. We're not interested
in conquest. We cannot do harm."

"You're doing a pretty good job of it."

"Job?" He looked at Sindona. "Oh. You and your friend.
I am sorry, but it is . . . necessary. You won't be harmed."

Quarnian could see he was telling the truth—as he saw it.
No physical harm would come to her, of course. But it
wasn't any picnic being kept prisoner.

"I don't understand," the captain said in answer to her
thought. "You'll have the run of the ship, eventually."

"Let me explain to her," Sindona jumped in. "We always
do what we're told on this ship. We have no choice
ourselves."

Quarnian could feel the stress of desperation in the last
five words. That was what Sindona hated, why she wanted
to leave the ship. She wanted a choice.

Quarnian tried not to laugh.

"You will be . . . set free now," Vorst said. "But only if
you don't try to escape. You must tell your friends that."

"And what if they don't want to stay?"

"You will persuade them."

Quarnian sighed. She wasn't really sure whether to
believe the captain's words about not doing them harm. She
looked to Sindona for a guide. Sindona nodded.

"All right," Quarnian said. "It's a deal."

"I hope you have some sort of plan," Quarnian said to
Sindona.

"Plan? No. You will have to remain. There's no choice."

Quarnian looked hard at her as she floated in front of her
eyes. "You didn't sound so . . ."

Sindona placed a finger to her lips.

Quarnian felt like kicking herself. Don't ask about plans; someone might overhear our thoughts. "I'll go along with your way," she said, stressing the words so Sindona would know she understood. From the captain's reactions, it looked as if he wasn't used to reading expressions in voices.

Sindona led her to more recognizable sections of the ship. Outside the archive room, she stopped. "I must go *now*," she said stiffly. Quarnian knew she'd be back. She tried not to think about it and give herself away.

Bruce and Rex were waiting inside. Bruce propelled himself to her. "Lady!"

"Where were you?" Rex asked.

Quarnian took a deep breath and began the explanation.

Chapter Thirteen

"I'm tired of being stuck here," Rex burst out. "We've got to do something."

Quarnian looked up from the archives and rubbed a hand over her face. There had been an undertone of tension in every movement Rex had made in the past few days, ever since she had told him about their situation. Part of it was because they were trapped, but there was another, more personal undertone, as though her very presence near him was the cause of it. She had ignored it for as long as she could, but she could tell it was hard on him. "What do you want to do?"

"Damn it, Quarn, you got us into this mess. You've got to get us out."

She didn't have the strength to remind him not to use that nickname. "Rex, I can't."

"So you want us to just accept it?"

Quarnian sighed. No one seemed to understand: when you have no choice, you have to accept things. She told herself dozens of times that her hunch might be wrong, but the words rang false. She knew better than to admit that to Rex. "There's just nothing I can do right now. I'm sorry."

"You're sorry? What the frast is that—"

"Rex, I was wrong. I got us into this mess, and it looks like there's no way out. It's my fault, I admit it. I'm sorry I got you into this, but that's all I *can* say." She turned quickly back to the screen; everything she saw was blurry with moisture.

Rex was silent for several moments. "Well," he said softly, "it was almost worth it to hear you admit that." There was a hint of a smile in his voice. "But we've got to do something. You've got to—"

"I can't. I still can't control my thoughts; the harder I try, the more I broadcast. If I wait until I can . . ."

"We might never get out of here."

Quarnian nodded slowly. "That's what I've been trying to tell you."

Rex cursed.

"I'm sorry, Rex—I know I keep saying that, but it's true. I . . . I like you and I never thought anything like this would happen."

"It's all right," Rex said softly. "I've been depending on you for everything; I've gotten out of the habit of thinking for myself. Now that you can't do anything, I guess I'll have to get all of us out of this mess." He smiled.

"You and Bruce."

"Bruce? I don't want to work with him."

"Please, Rex, we've gone over this. The crew isn't interested in Bruce; he can do things we can't."

"But . . ."

"Please, Rex."

Rex sighed. "All right. I'll keep you posted."

"Don't. I may give it all away."

Rex shrugged. "All right. I won't let you know unless you tell me to."

"Fine." Quarnian returned to the archives. "I'll see if there's anything helpful here. I'll talk to you at dinner."

There was no sound of departure behind her. "Quarnian," Rex said, his voice barely above a whisper.

She turned. "What is it?"

"I just wanted to say . . . I like you, too."

Quarnian felt an aching chill at the words. "Thank you,

Rex. I . . ." Her vocal cords didn't want to move; her throat felt filled with cotton. She was so alone, so charged with responsibility. She wanted someone to soothe it all away.

"Quarnian?"

It had been so long since she had relaxed, she realized, so long since she had had the comfort of another person's touch. And she had gotten to know Rex better than anyone else. He was, despite everything, a very attractive man. . . .

Quarnian made a decision. "Rex, I . . . I know I've discouraged you before. I always thought it would be a mistake. I might get trapped into feeling what I didn't dare feel. I was trying to guard against . . . against . . ."

"What are you talking about?"

"I feel so . . . so . . ." She looked away from the deck and into his eyes. "Rex, I'd like you to make love with me."

The words dropped with a thud. Quarnian could sense the sound of the stars passing by. And horrifyingly, she knew his answer.

"Quarn . . ."

"You don't want to." Was her face turning red? "You must think I've got a tremendous ego. Men tear themselves apart to go to bed with me; me granting you the privilege. I didn't mean it that way. I'm sorry . . ."

He shook his head. "That's not it. Look, Quarn, I like you too much. I know that sounds weird, but I guess I'm just a weird person. I like no strings attached as much as anyone, but not with . . . a friend. It seems funny, like we really should have more of a commitment. I like you too much to have sex with you. I couldn't unless I began to . . . love you. I don't. I'm sorry, but I don't think I could."

"You've been in love before?"

Rex's cheeks flushed. "Once. Twice. It was . . . well, you know the feelings."

"I don't," Quarnian said.

"What?"

"I don't let myself fall in love." She looked at her feet. "I don't want to be caught in a commitment."

There was a perfect silence in the room, as though it were one of those special chambers that damp all vibrations.

"I'm sorry," Rex said softly.

Quarnian forced a smile. "Now *you're* apologizing." It was probably for the best, anyway, she thought. Once they made love, it would be impossible to say no to Rex. "Let's end this conversation before we make bigger fools of ourselves. Find Bruce and get to work."

Slowly, reluctantly, Rex left.

Quarnian returned to the archives. She kept rereading the words, but nothing registered.

Why don't I get out of here? Quarnian thought. I've been staring at this thing too long. I should at least get a tour of my prison.

"Very good," came the voice behind her. "You read it all perfectly."

Quarnian turned. Sindona smiled at her. "How long have you—?"

"I just came in. I wanted to see if you could still receive me."

"I didn't hear. I guess there's nothing *to* hear. You don't have the luxury of hearing footsteps around here."

"Not if your feet don't touch the ground. Come on, let's take a tour; I managed to convince the captain to let you look around. But first, put these on. Your own ones are beginning to smell." She tossed a bundle to Quarnian.

Quarnian unfolded it; it was one of the ship's jumpsuits. She smiled. "Thanks. Although I'd like to take a shower first."

Sindona shook her head. "No need. A chemical in the suit will eliminate any dirt. We don't have the water to waste on washing."

Quarnian took a closer look at the cloth. It was light, but seemed to hold the heat of her hand with surprising efficiency. She suspected it was more than just that; that the suit had been designed to be the perfect cloth—warm, light, tear resistant, and long wearing.

"Exactly," Sindona said. "Well, go ahead, change. I'll meet you outside your cabin."

The change took longer than Quarnian would have liked. "Sorry to take so long," she said as she emerged. "I'm still not used to zero gee. I think I'm going to miss gravity."

"Don't worry. We'll get out of here. I'm the one who's going to have trouble adjusting."

"You seem so positive."

"Nothing is positive. But I'm going to give it a hell of a try. If you don't give us away, that is."

"I don't—"

"That's not a criticism. We're going to have to work on things. We'll talk as we look."

Sindona led her through the corridors, pointing out landmarks—a splotch of rust, a weld in the metal, a fire-extinguisher mount. "You're going to have to find your way around by yourself," she explained. "It'll be easier now that I'm not under orders to confuse you."

Quarnian tried to pay attention, but she knew she'd get lost easily for quite some time. She felt like an anthropologist among some tribe that knew every inch of its territory. "There have been some changes in the design, haven't there?"

Sindona looked at her. "You know?"

"Well, Bruce mentioned it."

"Yes. No one can stay in the same house for five hundred years without making a change or two. We've rearranged the furniture a bit. Sometimes we were forced to." She pointed toward the wall to their left; it had a makeshift look to it. "Most of that section depressurized ninety years ago. The wall seals it off."

"You mean there's vacuum on the other side?"

Sindona nodded. "Pure space. Oh, don't worry, it's safe enough."

"How safe is that?"

Sindona smiled. "We're very careful not to lose any of our crew. The trick, they say, is to hold your breath and close your eyes. Even a human can survive a little while that way."

"You treat it all very lightly."

Sindona's expression suddenly became serious. "No. I don't. It's our greatest fear—to be caught in a depressurization. It's drummed into our heads from the time we're children. Not all of us can survive vacuum; most of us aren't even tested for it." Her smile returned. "I'm sure you can guess why."

Quarnian smiled back. She liked her. Sindona had changed since the beginning. Even the way she talked. . . . "Why did you always used to pause when you were talking?"

"What?"

"You used to . . . I don't know, sort of stop in the middle of sentences. You haven't been doing that lately."

"Oh, that? I was being closely monitored; they kept breaking in to tell me what to say. Now they don't care."

"Does that mean . . . ?"

"We're going to have to be careful; they still don't trust us. But they have more important things to do than to watch everything we do. Now, what do you want to see first, the hydroponics or the lab?"

Quarnian chose the hydroponics.

She nearly got a headache when she stepped inside the door. It was too bright with a cold fluorescent glare that contrasted completely with the dimness of the rest of the ship. The air was warmer, too; filled with odd but delicious aromas that made her mouth water. They were unfamiliar combinations, smelling of wine and oranges, with hints of grilled steak and fish.

The room looked the size of a football field. It was cylindrical; Quarnian guessed they were near the axis of the ship. A giant column of light ran down its length, and around the curving walls were rows and rows of green, with a patch of other colors here and there.

"It's enormous," Quarnian said.

Once again, the smile returned to Sindona's face; it looked very natural there. "One of the few areas we haven't modified. Except for improvements on the light column, of course. What would you like to look at first? Fruit, vegetables, meat—you name it."

"You have livestock in here, too?"

"Follow me," was Sindona's only answer.

She led Quarnian along the rows. Quarnian looked at the plants, trying to place them. Some were easy—potatoes

looked like potatoes, corn like corn. Some weren't: that
grayish purple swelling on the plant that looked like a carrot
top. The brown tomatoes. She frowned. They couldn't have
been decorative, but how had it happened? Random muta-
tion? Or fancy crossbreeding?

"It's a mixture of both," Sindona said.

Her voice startled Quarnian. "Don't do that."

"If I didn't, you'd never know that you're sending."

She was right, but it annoyed Quarnian. She was used to
being in control of a situation, but she had lost control the
second she had set foot on the *Staroamer*. She hadn't ever
felt this helpless.

"Here we are," Sindona said.

The plants she pointed to were small and bushy, with tiny
flowers like bells. "What are they?"

"They're not ripe now. They produce a fruit about the
size of your fist. Once cooked, they taste a lot like steak."

"How do you know?"

Sindona laughed. "You're right. The last bit of real meat
was eaten here about four hundred years ago. You'll have to
give it a try and tell us."

"Why haven't they . . . ?" Quarnian shook her head.
"You didn't want to feed us anything too unfamiliar until
you were sure we were going to stay. Did I think that or did
you?"

"A little of both, I think. Don't worry, Quarnian, you'll
get used to it. It won't take long once we get started. I'm as
anxious to get out of here as you are, remember?"

The lingering doubt returned; Quarnian didn't know
whether to believe her. Once again, she cursed the
undependability of the Training.

"Don't think about that," Sindona whispered. She looked
around quickly. "I don't think anyone received that. But
your Training could be your ace in the hole."

"What difference does it make? I'll just give everything
away. I bet a baby around here could do better at keeping
thoughts secret."

"You do more than just send and receive; you probably
can receive emotions from non-mindspeakers. But we'll have
to discuss it later. Someone's—"

"Lady!"

Quarnian tried to turn, but her feet were too far from a solid surface for her to move easily. Bruce flowed by her to face her; he was smiling.

"You're moving well," she said. "I thought you didn't like free-fall."

"You get used to it. You all right?"

"Fine." She looked at Sindona; the white-haired woman had discreetly turned away. It annoyed Quarnian; she'd be able to read the conversation anyway. "Bruce, have you talked with Rex?"

Bruce's scowl was his only answer.

"Talk with him. You two are going to have to work things out."

"Don't like him."

The words were a condemnation. "Do it for me, Bruce."

"Why?"

"He'll explain everything." Quarnian didn't want to have to say too much. "Just do as I tell you."

Bruce shrugged. "OK," he said, sounding as though his day had been ruined. He pushed off and swam away from them.

"Good idea," Sindona said.

Quarnian suppressed her annoyance. It wasn't Sindona's fault she could pick up just about everything Quarnian thought. In some ways it was a good thing—if Sindona couldn't pick up something, no one else could.

"What next?" Sindona asked.

"Might as well get the rest of the bad news," Quarnian said. "Let's see your laboratory."

"Better be prepared," Sindona said as they reached the door to the lab. "Our science is as advanced as our evolution."

"So I guessed." Quarnian had concentrated on landmarks the entire route; her instincts told her they might come in handy later.

They entered the room. For the first time aboard ship, Quarnian saw something resembling clutter. Instruments floated in the air, kept handy by short lengths of wire or string. Burners stuck out of the walls like candles on tenta-cles. Quarnian had the impression that they'd be dangerous if not properly handled. Over in one corner was a CRT, in much better repair than Sindona's terminal (a guide to priorities aboard ship).

The woman in the lab reminded Quarnian of a skinny Santa Claus, with her smile and forced jollity. Her hair was the same color as the rest of the crew's. Quarnian was beginning to tire of shades of blond and white.

"You will get used to it," the woman said.

"What?"

"Our hair. You were thinking of that."

Quarnian sighed.

"My name is Addra," the woman went on. "No, Sindona, don't coach me until I ask you to. I want to see if I know the old tongue." She smiled at Quarnian. "It seems so strange to use sound to communicate. Am I doing well?"

"Very well," Quarnian said. "I've got a few questions to ask you."

"Ask. I'll tell you almost anything."

"Almost?"

Addra laughed, a slow giggle that grated on Quarnian's ears. "Almost. But ask."

"What do you do here?"

"What science? All. Biology, chemistry, even physics." She pronounced the last word with a long y.

"What's your specialty?"

"Specialty?" She looked at Sindona. "Oh. We can't afford specialties here. I prefer biology, though. We can't just depend on mu—mutations."

"Is that why you've managed to advance so much?"

"Sure. Oh, natural mutations were what we depended on in the beginning. But in the past hundred years we've been helping nature along a little."

"Is that why some of you don't need air?"

Addra looked at Sindona again and Quarnian realized she had asked the wrong question. She got the distinct impression of a scolding, one that Sindona was accepting meekly.

"Let's switch to something else," Quarnian said quickly.

"Those guns—the ones they used on me. How do they work?"

"The epilyzer?" Another look to Sindona and the smile was back. "Electricity. It creates a state of electric discharge in the brain, sort of an ... epileptic seizure."

"Very effective," Quarnian commented. "I'd like to get a tour now."

It proved a wise move. Addra was like any other human: happy to show off where she worked. Quarnian didn't pay much attention. The tour concentrated on biology: gene experiments, mostly. Quarnian acted fascinated as she listened to how the steaks were invented.

Physics was next.

"I'm trying to find the fourth method of FTL travel," Addra said with casual excitement.

The casual part scared Quarnian. "I thought there was only one way."

A big-toothed smile greeted her. "There are three so far. I'm not surprised. Once you have one, there's not much ... incentive to invent any others."

"But why didn't you use one of the methods to find a planet?"

The smile was indulgent now; Quarnian knew Addra's words before she opened her mouth: by the time they had discovered warp, they were committed to their genetic journey.

Addra looked puzzled. "I didn't know you could receive, too."

"She can," Sindona broke in quickly. "But it's too sporadic to be usable."

"Oh," Addra said. There was doubt in her voice.

Another good time to change the subject. "You mentioned chemistry," Quarnian broke in. "What have you been doing there?"

"I ... I'm afraid I don't have the time to talk with you anymore. I'll have to explain some other time." She smiled. "There's no hurry."

But there is a hurry to get me out of here, Quarnian thought. She didn't say anything; it was likely Addra overheard her suspicion. Quietly, she and Sindona left the lab.

"Why'd she kick us out of there like that?" Quarnian asked as they made their way through the corridors.

"I don't know," Sindona said. "I couldn't receive anything; I don't think she trusts me. All I can guess is that they're planning something they don't want you to know about."

"Thanks. You're a big help."

Sindona smiled. "All right, you knew that already. Anything else you want to see?"

Quarnian shook her head. She had had enough of exploring for a while. She wanted just to rest and let Rex figure a way out of this.

"Please try not to think about that," Sindona said. "Someone else might overhear."

"All right," Quarnian snapped.

Sindona seemed to know enough not to pursue the issue. "I'll take you back to your cabin, if you want. You'll be able to relax a little. You look tense."

Quarnian smiled. "My stomach feels like it's permanently tense. I could use some time to try to calm down. What are you going to do?"

Sindona looked embarrassed. "I . . . I'm going to . . . see Rex."

"You say that as though you're hiding something."

"No, I . . ."

And suddenly the thought bloomed in Quarnian's mind: she was going to make love to him. "Sindona," she began, feeling the tenseness redouble, "are you . . . ?"

"I'm sorry, Quarnian, I really am. I was ordered to. His genes and mine . . . Well, I can't disobey an order without attracting suspicion. Believe me, if there was any way . . ."

"All right. Enough. You and Rex are adults. I'm sure he won't mind. You think I care what the two of you do?"

"I thought—"

"What Rex does is his own business," Quarnian said.

"But you . . . Oh, never mind. I made a mistake, I guess."

"Fine. Do whatever you want. I'm going back to my cabin."

"Let me show you."

"I think I can find my way. I can't depend on you all the time." Quarnian pushed off for her room.

Chapter Fourteen

One bad thing about weightlessness, Quarnian thought. You can't pace.

Pushing off each of the walls was a poor substitute; she quickly began to feel like a Ping-Pong ball. Kicking things was no substitute, either. Newton's Law sent her flying in the opposite direction; the reaction was often worse than the action.

The dimness and drabness of the room oppressed her further. Is this what she had to look forward to? A lifetime of bare metal walls and semidarkness? A stranger trapped among half-aliens? An existence of being indoctrinated into their evolutionary plan until she accepted it?

Yes.

She was going to stay here for the rest of her life. She knew it. The hunch was stronger than any she had ever had before.

They couldn't escape; there was no way they could refill the *Wreckless*. Rex would be swayed by Sindona; he wouldn't plan a thing. She'd have to do it all, every one of her thoughts inches from being detected. It would never work.

You've never been such a pessimist before, she told herself.

But you've never been so helpless before, came the answer.

Quarnian felt the need to cry. She shook her head before her eyes could mist. Tears wouldn't help.

Face it. You're going to have to live with it.

The thought had an unfortunate ring of comfort. She elaborated on it. Accept the inevitable. Try to—

Someone knocked on the door. Quarnian opened it listlessly.

One of the crew, the man with the red-tinged hair who had let her out of her cell, floated in the doorway, an odd expression on his puffy face. There was something about him, something unpleasant that went beyond his appearance. Quarnian couldn't put her finger on it; all she knew was that she didn't want to talk with him.

She sighed. "I suppose the captain wants to see me."

He shook his head. "Come in?" His voice still sounded a tiny bit screechy. It grated on her nerves.

She shrugged and let him pass. "What do you want?"

"The journey is important. We must all contribute."

Quarnian shook her head. "I'm not in the mood to contribute anything right now."

"You must. I was selected."

"Selected? What for?"

"For you."

Quarnian felt a chill. "I don't understand," she lied.

"Our . . . genes must be . . . joined. Mated."

"Not now," Quarnian said with a sigh. "Maybe later, when I'm used to the idea. I don't even know your name."

"I am Taril. The captain has—"

"I don't care what the captain says. I've got a right to my own choice."

The man looked at her as though the idea was alien to him. "The captain—"

"I don't care." Quarnian tried to size the man up. He was only about her size, and didn't look particularly strong. She didn't want to have to give a demonstration of what she could do once she found his weak spot, but if he tried anything, she wouldn't hesitate to use her knowledge. She found the spot on the side of his neck, just behind the left jugular. Pattern three should do it.

"You will let it happen. For the good of the ship."

"Get out of here." Quarnian wondered why they had chosen him for her. It couldn't be because of his looks; she found him repellant. He might have had the right genes, but as far as she was concerned, he had nothing she liked. "Leave me alone."

Taril pulled out an atomizer from the pocket of his jumpsuit. "I must use this." He pressed the bulb hard between his fingers.

"What . . . ?" A fine mist spread out at her and surrounded her like a cloud, too quickly for her to avoid it. She tried to hold her breath, but the aroma burrowed up her nose despite her best efforts.

It was vaguely familiar and very pleasant. She sniffed it in deeply, just to identify it, she told herself.

The deep, musky scent grew stronger. Now she was drinking it in, unable to stop. It was very pleasant.

She began to feel herself relaxing; the knot in her stomach untied. She became more aware of her body. There was a pleasantly aching tingle in her skin. She felt an urgent need to be touched: on her lips, on her neck, along her breasts, yes, even . . .

She looked at the man in front of her. Why hadn't she noticed before how handsome he was? His smile seemed so attractive, his lips so sensual. She could see his tongue moving behind his teeth, and the sight brought to mind fascinating possibilities. Her eyes moved down his body, and she began to wonder what he would look like without his jumpsuit. She imagined him naked beside her, his soft hands gently massaging the tingling parts of her body.

She wanted him to massage her, to move his hands and lips along her, making her ready, and then, at the proper moment . . .

"No!" Quarnian screeched. She *wanted* to make love to him; that was what terrified her.

He began to undo his jumpsuit.

"Stop that!" The screamed-out words barely dampened

her artificial desire. She was just on the edge; the slightest
extra sexual stimulus and she would lose all control.

The man looked puzzled. "You don't mean that."

His voice was still the same, but now it sounded like
gentle music. Why was she resisting? "Get out of here!" She
desired him intensely and hated him for it. She'd paralyze
him, kill him . . .

But she didn't trust herself to touch him.

"Get *out*!" she shouted again. Her anger seemed to
weaken her desire. But it wasn't enough; the urge to submit
was too strong. She needed something to replace her passion
with rage.

She closed her eyes. Henri Zwiko and his goddamned
dreamstone.

The memories flooded back, surprisingly vivid after eight
years of trying to bury them. Every minute of that evening,
from the moment she saw him, fat and balding and smelling
of garlic, laughing too loudly at his own jokes as he enter-
tained his guests. She had gone to him, practically throwing
herself at his feet, guided by her intuition and still trusting it
implicitly to keep her safe. And he had taken the bait,
grunting in pleasure as he offered to show her more of his
mansion. Like the bedroom. . . .

Her pleasant fumblings of adolescent sex were no prepa-
ration. He had taken her quickly and roughly, before she
was ready, causing her to gasp as pain imploded inside her.
He had believed her cry was one of pleasure and collapsed
on her, smiling, satisfied, pressing her roughly beneath him,
the stubble of his beard like sandpaper against her skin. She
had wanted to run screaming from him, to claw the skin
from his back, but could not, made helpless by an instinct
that shouted at her to wait for him to sleep soundly, so she
could search for what she later discovered was the dreamstone that she needed to save a world. And silent tears had
run down her cheeks at her helplessness.

Her rage was now a white hot flame, burning through all
other considerations. She looked at Taril and imagined
Zwiko's face and the smell of garlic. "Get out or I'll kill
you!" She had never meant the threat more than now.

Taril looked baffled. He glanced at the spray bottle, as though deciding if he should use it again.

Despite the strength her anger gave her, Quarnian wasn't sure she could resist the chemical again. *It won't work,* she thought, trying to hide her desperation. *I'll overcome it like I did this time.*

He started; evidently he had received her. *Get out!* Quarnian thought. *Get out get out getout getoutgetoutgetout—*

Taril took another look at the atomizer, then at her. Then, with a puzzled slowness, he turned and left the room. Each instant until the door shut seemed to take years.

Quarnian quickly locked the door, panting short, sexual gulps of air. She was a burning red sun of anger.

Was that what she was about to accept? A life of being treated that way?

Her answer was a ringing no.

"If they're going to want me here," she whispered to herself, "they're going to have to fight to keep me."

Her emotions had cooled; it was time to take action. No depending on Rex to come up with something. She had always depended on herself before, herself and her luck. She'd go back to depending on them again.

Feeling almost normal, she snapped open the door and went to find Rex. Sindona or no Sindona, they were getting out of there.

Quarnian pounded on Rex's door; she didn't care if she was interrupting anything. In fact, she rather hoped she was.

It opened quickly. "Quarn? What are you . . . ?"

She pushed by him into the room. There was no sign of anyone else. "When'd Sindona leave?"

"She hasn't been here." Rex looked puzzled. "Is something wrong? Your voice sounds strange."

"I'm fine. Have you figured a way out yet?"

"I thought you told me not to tell you."

"I changed my mind. Did you talk with Bruce?"

"Couldn't find him. I don't know where he is."

Quarnian cursed.

"Quarn? What happened? You're acting strange."

Her eyes stopped darting around the room and lit on his face.

And the feeling returned.

"No," she whispered. "No."

Rex's face was filled with concern; she felt it pulling her like a black hole. "No, what?" he asked.

"They've done something to me." His hands looked so gentle, so strong. He was the one who could . . . No, she must resist.

"Done something?" He moved (no, no!) nearer. "What?"

His face was too close, his mouth too inviting. She could resist no longer. She leaped for him, lips hungering for his.

"Quarn . . ."

She was tearing at her jumpsuit. "Please, Rex," she said breathlessly, "can't help . . ."

She could say no more; the words were getting in the way of her needs.

She gave in to them.

She didn't know how long she floated in his arms. She felt drained and exhausted, with none of the fulfilling feeling sex usually brought her. But her frightening desire had ended.

She stirred. Zero-gee sex sounded better in theory than it turned out; humans needed to brace themselves against something. And it was messy.

Rex's eyes were closed. She wondered if he had fallen asleep. "Rex?"

The eyes popped open.

"Rex, I'm sorry."

Rex smiled lazily. "No need to apologize. You were terrific."

"I'm not looking for compliments. It wasn't my idea."

"It wasn't?" A tiny bit of disappointment crept into the words. "What do you mean?"

She explained about the spray and its effect on her.

"What? You mean you didn't want to?"

"Rex, I couldn't control myself."

"You could have told me," Rex grumbled.

Quarnian looked at him, horrified at the indignation in his tone. "What's the matter, Rex? Doesn't this one count?"

Rex reddened. "Quarn, I didn't mean—"

"You sure as frast did! Don't you have any idea how much this frightens me? Or are you only interested in your own ego?"

Rex floated in front of her, unable to meet her hard gaze. She could see the glimmering of contrition on his face. She waited.

"I'm sorry, Quarn." His voice was different, with less swagger and more friendship. "I didn't realize."

"No. You don't know how . . . how horrible it was. You have no idea." She swallowed back the beginning of tears. "I'll get those bastards for that. I'll wreck their goddamned ship!"

"All right, Quarn, calm down. It's over."

"Don't treat me like a child!"

"All right, all right. Just relax. I want to get out of here just as much as you do."

"Not nearly as much." Quarnian swallowed again. "I'm sorry I bothered you this way. I couldn't help—"

"It's all right. I suppose I've fantasized about a woman who . . . No, that's insensitive. I guess it was hell for you."

"I'd rather not talk about it anymore. And this isn't a precedent. I didn't want to do it."

Rex nodded. "I understand."

She looked at him closely; his words sounded too much like his "We won't if you don't want to" line. But she could read it was the truth. And, she realized, his claim that he couldn't have sex with a friend was a lie.

She shook her head. No, that was too cruel—he meant it when he said it. Only a syron could see that it was not the truth, merely the way he managed to keep from getting too involved. She had her tricks, he had his.

"All right," Quarnian said. She was beginning to feel a bit better.

"Why were you asking for Sindona here?"

"I . . . I thought she might have dropped by."

Rex snorted. "What's the real reason?"

It took her a moment to gather the strength to say the words. "She was supposed . . . to be doing the same thing with you."

"Spray me with that stuff? Why'd you let it happen to you if—"

"I *didn't* know. She didn't mention it to me," Quarnian said quietly. "I don't think she thought she'd need it."

Rex turned rose pink. "I guess she's right."

"You guess?"

Rex broke into a feeble grin. "All right, it was obvious. But I'm a normal, healthy man. I have desires."

"Too many of them. You think with your crotch."

"Well, you were the one who . . ." Rex stopped. "Look, let's drop the subject before we both say things we'll regret. Tell you what. I won't look at another woman unless you approve."

"That's not—"

Someone knocked. "Rex? Quarnian?" came Sindona's voice, muffled by the door. "Let me in."

They scrambled for their clothes and opened the door.

"Are you all right?" Sindona asked. "I came here as soon as I heard, but I realized I'd better not disturb you."

"Why weren't you here?" Quarnian asked, suspicious again. Sindona must have known about the chemical she had been sprayed with.

"They stopped me before I could get here. Wanted to know how much I had told you. While I was lying my way out of it, Taril came in. He told them what happened."

"What was it?" Quarnian asked.

"A pheromone spray. It was tailored to your sexual reflexes—they got them when they tested your blood. They were amazed you were able to resist it."

"I didn't," Quarnian mumbled.

Sindona looked around the room. "So I guessed. It was a tremendous achievement to hold out as long as you did. Congratulations."

"Thanks."

"I didn't know, Quarnian, believe me. I had no idea they were planning it so soon. It was too crazy."

Quarnian said nothing.

Rex jumped into the silence. "That stuff could be awfully dangerous if it got to New Wichatah. I know men . . ."

"It has to be different for each person; you can't mass-produce it." Sindona turned back to Quarnian. "I'm sorry this happened. If I had known, I would have warned you. Believe me. But we can't worry about that. We have other problems."

"Like what?" Quarnian snapped.

"Like, why do you think they decided to do it now?"

"I don't know. They were in a hurry."

"Yes. And for one specific thing. Why do they want to keep you here?"

"To . . ." Quarnian stopped. "My God," she whispered.

"Exactly. They determined this was your most fertile time."

"My God," Quarnian repeated, dazed. "Damn it, I can't get pregnant. It might—"

Rex cleared his throat. "It won't happen. I've had sperase shots. I'll be sterile for another three months."

Quarnian looked at him, wondering whether it was incredible luck or just a soothing lie. "You what?"

"There are awfully stringent laws against leaving a child without a father in New Wichatah. It's best to avoid the possibility."

Of course, Quarnian realized. It had to be true. She had offered to make love to him earlier that day; if there had been any danger of pregnancy, her instincts would never have told her it was all right.

Sindona laughed. "I'll be sure to tell the captain. But in a few days; that should give Quarnian a month of safety. They're going to try to improve the pheromone spray, you know."

"I'm not surprised. Which means we have a month. We're going to have to get to work."

"Fine. Where do we start?" Rex asked.

Quarnian looked at Sindona. She was just going to have to trust her. "We begin with lessons. Teach me how to keep my thoughts to myself."

Chapter Fifteen

"Ready to begin?" Sindona asked.

Quarnian nodded. Somehow, Sindona had convinced Vorst to let them work together in the archive room. Theoretically, Quarnian was learning about the ship. "Will anyone receive us?"

"Not unless they're nearby. You don't send indefinitely; the projection becomes fainter with distance."

"Thank the stars for that."

"In more ways than you mean. If it didn't fade out, we'd get everyone's thoughts at once. It's bad enough that it travels through the walls."

"Well, what do you want me to do?"

Sindona shrugged. "I can't explain exactly. . . ."

"Some teacher you are."

Sindona didn't appear upset by the snapped-out words. "It's something you feel rather than learn. Either you have it or you don't."

"So what's the point?"

"I can guide you. Please, Quarnian. I want to get out of here as much as you do."

Quarnian took a deep breath. Her frustration was shortening her temper. "Give me a hint?"

"I'll see what I can do. Let's go back to receiving. Now, relax your mind. . . . "

Quarnian did everything Sindona suggested. She thought of nothing; sure enough, Sindona's thoughts slipped into her mind. At first she still couldn't tell them from her own. Then she began to notice something about them, an overtone she couldn't put a finger on. It was . . . as if they were in a slightly different voice. It wasn't Sindona's, but it wasn't the voice she usually heard in her head. The difference wasn't one of tone, or pitch, or expression; the thoughts *felt* different in a way she couldn't describe.

That's enough for now, Sindona thought after an hour's worth of work.

Quarnian protested, "I'm beginning to get the hang of it. I've got to move on to . . ."

"I can't stay much longer. Listen. With your mind."

Quarnian tried. Nothing. . . . No, wait. Someone thinking Sindona's name.

"You've got it; they'll be after me in a minute. I have other duties here; they don't like me spending so much time helping you. I'm afraid it'll have to wait."

"But . . ."

"Let Rex and Bruce handle things for a little while. I can't help you gain control today, anyway. It's the hardest thing to learn. Children around here project everything; it takes them years to get in control." She smiled. "It won't take you that long, but we can't rush things. We can't expect miracles."

Quarnian sighed. "You're the boss, I guess."

"Only when it comes to these lessons." Sindona smiled and left her alone.

The lessons were always too short.

"All right, try it again. You projected most of that."

Quarnian tried again. And again. Think of something, anything. Only don't project it; don't put it into the corner of my mind, where it will be broadcast to others. The whole idea was frustrating; everything she thought was repeated back to her by Sindona.

Not every one, Sindona thought.

At least Quarnian was now able to tell what thoughts weren't her own. *Almost.*

Quiet. You're trying too hard not to project. Soften your ideas; don't let them escape. Put them in another part of your brain.

Quarnian tried again with another thought.

Sindona repeated it back.

Another attempt, another repeat.

The days passed. Two, three, five. She wanted to know what Rex and Bruce were doing; to help guide them and suggest options. She began to have the feeling there was some sort of trouble, even more than they had expected.

On the sixth day, tired and frustrated, she thought a long list of obscenities at Sindona.

Don't blame me, Sindona thought.

Quarnian rubbed her forehead. She felt she deserved a headache. Sindona was an implacable teacher; this was harder than anything she had tried before. And that included her Training. Her mind drifted back to those days, the work, the testing. The day she was told she'd be a gold star. And the rest of her life—trooping around the universe, ending up here. She shook her head.

And she realized Sindona hadn't thought anything back to her.

Penny for your thoughts.

"You know, I . . ." Quarnian said aloud; speaking was still more natural for her. "Do you mean . . . ?"

Sindona was smiling broadly. "You did it."

"Seriously?"

"Seriously."

"But how . . . ?"

"Try it again. Put your mind in the same frame you had it in then."

Quarnian tried to follow the instructions. Count to ten, she thought. One, two, three . . .

"I heard two and three. Not one."

Another try.

Sindona shook her head. "No good. I received it all."

Quarnian tried desperately to recapture the state she had been in. She couldn't; it was too hard to duplicate her thinking process.

"We're making progress," Sindona said. "You'll get it soon enough."

Quarnian insisted on total concentration during the drills; she was not very happy when Rex interrupted them.

"Sorry," he said, bursting through the door just as Quarnian had failed five straight attempts to keep her mind shut. "I—"

"Rex!" Quarnian shouted. "Get out of here!"

"But—"

"Later!"

"Damn it, it's important!"

"Now wait a minute, you two," Sindona burst in.

Quarnian ignored her. "What could be so important?"

"Bruce is gone."

Quarnian felt her anger deflating like a popped balloon. "Gone? That's ridiculous. He's got to be on the ship."

Rex shrugged. "You're right—only I can't find him. His room hasn't been used; I don't think he's been there for days."

Quarnian looked at Sindona; she felt sick inside. "Could the captain have done anything to him?"

Sindona shrugged. "I haven't heard anything about it."

"You're avoiding the answer. He didn't like Bruce's looks. He'd just be another mouth to feed."

"I don't know."

Quarnian didn't like the way she said it. "You think it's possible."

Sindona looked surprised. "I know I didn't let that thought slip."

Quarnian enjoyed her confusion. "You didn't," she said; it was the only explanation she was going to give. "Rex, see if you can find anything."

"I've been trying. . . ."

"Well, try again. Sindona will see what she can find out."

Sindona pushed off toward the door. "Right. I'll . . ."

"Not now. After the lesson. Rex, get to work. And try to get something accomplished. I don't want to have to do everything myself."

Rex sullenly left the room.

"You really shouldn't boss him around like that," Sindona said. "He doesn't like it."

"I don't give a damn what he likes."

"Yes, you do."

Quarnian looked at Sindona; she was smiling mysteriously. "What the frast are you talking about?"

"Never mind," Sindona said. "Back to your lesson. Try to hide a thought from me."

Slowly, it began to come. The lessons became shorter; hours stolen from Sindona's free time. She had the feeling that Vorst was beginning to catch on.

First one thought, then two, then several—Quarnian began to learn how to keep secrets.

But too slowly; she had to concentrate on every thought. And she was missing the key ingredient: consistency.

And still there was no word about Bruce.

"Tell me the truth, Sindona," Quarnian said, her mind weary from all the days of practice. "How am I doing?"

"I don't know."

"Thanks."

"I meant it as a compliment. Look, Quarnian, you're asking me to teach you in two weeks what it took me a lifetime to learn." Sindona smiled and switched to mind-speech. *You shouldn't be asking out loud, anyway. This is a lesson.*

Quarnian sighed. All she wanted to do was shield her thoughts; she didn't plan to have to talk this way.

It has its uses, came the thought in her mind.

I can't keep more than half my ideas to myself.

That's half more than you used to. Keep trying.

Quarnian shook her head. *I have to get out of here. I used to see something besides these walls.*

The observatory.

The thought startled her. "Where's that?" Quarnian asked.

You'll never get anywhere if you—

"I'm tired of thinking at you. I'd just like to hear the sound of a voice for a change. Let's take a look at this observatory."

Sindona smiled. "I guess I have been overzealous. All right, the observatory it is." She led Quarnian into the corridors.

They headed to the bow of the ship.

The observatory door opened with a moan. The inside was covered with a layer of dust. It looked as though it hadn't been used in years.

The room was a bisected circle ten meters across, quite a change from the closets that passed for quarters in the rest of the ship. It was dominated by a glass wall that gave a full view of the stars in front of them.

Quarnian glided through the room, dust eddying in the air currents behind her. "I guess you don't come here too often."

Sindona nodded. "No one cares too much to look at the stars."

Quarnian understood as she stared out into the blackness. You couldn't get claustrophobic when you had no frame of reference, but when you looked outside, you yearned for space.

Sindona laughed.

"What's so funny?"

"I'm sorry, Quarnian. It's just that you've got it all wrong. We don't mind one way or another whether we're inside or out; it's the only thing we know."

"You weren't supposed to hear that."

"But you switched into the projecting mode. You've got to remember—"

"All right. We're here because I'm tired of lessons." Quarnian stared out the window; it was designed so she could look back along the length of the *Staroamer*. Out to the left, she thought she saw a disk among the pinpoints. New Wichatah? She felt sure of it. I wish, she thought, keeping rein on it as Sindona had taught her, I wish I were there. I wish I never had these infernal hunches. I wish—oh,

I don't *care* if you hear me, Sindona—I wish I could ditch you and find a way out of here.

Sindona gave no reaction to the thought; Quarnian knew she hadn't received it.

Well, it's some help, Quarnian thought (to herself!) as she stared into space.

A movement caught the corner of her eye.

She turned. A figure was moving along the side of the ship, tethered to a guide rope, examining for something.

There was something odd about it; after watching so many others float around the corridors like that, it took her a second to put her finger on it.

Her head nearly burst with the realization.

"He's got no spacesuit! He'll die!" The instant the words left her mouth, Quarnian realized the ridiculousness of them. He was moving slowly and deliberately, engrossed in the task, unbothered by the vacuum around him. She remembered what Sindona had told her: some of them had evolved further.

She stared out the window, feeling foolish. But it was one thing hearing about this; another to see it. It was overwhelming. How was she . . . ?

She recalled the pheromone spray; the thought of it always kept her away from despair. She was going to get out of here, or die trying. She meant the last words.

The door squeaked behind them. "What . . . ?" came a voice, exploding in anger. They turned.

It was Bruce.

"Shut the door," he shouted. "Dangerous." He pointed to the observatory glass.

"Bruce, where have you been?" Quarnian asked. The outburst surprised her; Bruce was almost garrulous. "Rex has been looking all over for you."

"Too bad."

"Bruce, we're not going to get out of here if you don't—"

"Not going."

"What do you mean, you're not going?" There was a queasy feeling in the pit of Quarnian's stomach: he meant it.

"Staying."

"Bruce, you can't . . ." She looked at Sindona and

remembered Bruce's feelings about her. *Could you leave us alone?* Quarnian thought.

Sindona left the room.

"Now, Bruce, you know you can't stay here. It's . . ." And suddenly Quarnian knew all her talk would do no good. Bruce's mind was made up. "Why?" she asked.

He looked up at her with hooded eyes. "You know."

And she realized she did: New Wichatah was his home in name only. She had promised him another world; he'd take this one. Bruce knew everything about the *Staroamer*; of course he would want to stay. "This is your home," she said.

A flicker of a smile played over his lips. "You understand."

An image filled her mind: Bruce growing up on New Wichatah, left alone because of his looks, spending all his time thinking about the *Staroamer*. It was his dream of escape, his way to leave the mundane and be swallowed up in space. He had been afraid when he first got here, but time had revived his dream.

"All right, Bruce. I suppose you know what's best for you. We won't force you to come along. But we can still use your help."

He shook his head. "No."

"But, why?"

"Member of the crew now. Wouldn't like it if . . . I . . . helped you escape."

Quarnian sighed; he had a point. "I suppose, then, you'll tell them everything."

Bruce looked up at her, startled. "No. Will not stop you, lady. You don't want to stay; you can go. But won't help."

She looked at him, trying to see if he could be trusted. Her hunch said yes. "All right, Bruce. And . . . thanks."

Bruce's eyes aimed downward. "Thanks to you, lady. You brought me here." He indicated the door; Quarnian went out and let him seal it.

"Well?" Sindona asked after Bruce disappeared down the corridor. "What did he say?"

"He . . . Wait a minute. Didn't you eavesdrop on me?"

"I tried to. Couldn't read a thing. I haven't gotten a thing from you since that thought about claustrophobia."

"Well," Quarnian said, "at least something's going right."

Chapter Sixteen

"And you just let him? Damn it, we're going to need—"

"I let him, Rex," Quarnian shouted back, matching him decibel for decibel. "We'll get along without him."

"But why?"

"What do you want me to do? Argue with him? I don't think words mean much to Bruce."

"You could have knocked him out or something. Brought him back here so we can knock some sense into him."

"And have him tell the crew the first chance he gets? He's going to leave us alone. Be thankful for that."

Rex glared at her, his anger defused by Quarnian's reflecting it back to him. She had let him rage on before speaking, to draw some of it off so he'd listen to her logic. She could tell he was about to accept it; but she knew he was unwilling.

Rex was breathing in short, angry gasps; his face was ruddy from the shouting. "I don't understand you. You want to get out of here—and you said yourself we need his help. You didn't do nearly enough to keep him with us."

Quarnian sighed. "I know. But I felt I had to let him have his way."

"Your feelings—"

"Yes," Quarnian snapped, "they *have* been wrong before. You've been complaining about that ever since I got here. They've done me pretty well so far; I'm going to stick with them."

The outburst did her good; she didn't mention she doubted they were going to get out.

Rex stared.

"Besides," she said more softly, "I think . . . I think that maybe that's the reason we're here. To give Bruce a home."

"That's all fine for him, but where does that leave us? Don't tell me you syrons always come up with the jackpot."

The jackpot. Quarnian felt bitter. She never hit any jackpot. Everything she did was only temporary. Others might benefit, but she just moved along. "Rex," she said, "I'm not going to explain the way I feel. I just . . . just have a hunch we're going to get out of here."

"We are?"

Quarnian had never gotten the hang of lying. "We are," she said, then moved quickly to another subject. "The good news is that we can begin talking about everything. Sindona passed me. What has to be done?"

"Other than everything?"

She smiled; he was over his anger now. She was happy about that. "First things first."

Rex thought for a moment. "I suppose I should take a look at the *Wreckless*. I was too excited to check for damage when I saw Bruce had . . . I mean, when I saw the air was gone. They may have wrecked things. I'd like to see if we have to make repairs."

Quarnian nodded. "Good. I'll talk with Sindona. Maybe she has some suggestions." She spun off a wall and glided toward the door between Rex's room and the corridor.

"Quarn, just one more thing."

She turned, impatient at the delay. "What?"

Rex looked embarrassed. "I . . . I'm sorry I lost my temper." The words came out grudgingly.

Quarnian smiled. "You look like a teenager. I expected you to."

He smiled back sheepishly. "You read me pretty well, don't you?"

"Comes with the territory." She floated out of the room.

"There," Sindona said as she pointed to the wire in the airlock control panel. "That should disconnect the alarm."

"Should?" Rex asked.

"For a few minutes. Get going."

Quarnian watched as Rex sealed on his helmet. Somehow, Sindona had found two of their suits. But time was important; if the crew discovered the suits were missing, they'd know exactly where to look for them. Quarnian held the second suit. She had planned to go out, too, but in the dimness of wherever they'd been stored, Sindona had picked the wrong one. It was Bruce's, too small for anyone else.

Rex nodded, the signal he was ready.

Sindona slipped the wire, then quickly hit the airlock door.

Rex jumped in, and it closed behind him.

Quarnian felt uncomfortable. Sindona controlled the lock, Rex did the exploring. She had somehow been given the responsibility for the worrying.

"He's out," Sindona reported.

Quarnian nodded. Sindona had advised against mind-speaking; their whispered voice wouldn't carry as far as their thoughts.

The moments oozed along. Quarnian checked her watch. Rex had been out there less than two minutes; he probably hadn't even reached the *Wreckless* yet. But it seemed like ages.

"Calm down," Sindona hissed. "You're beginning to project your thoughts."

"I . . ."

"Start talking. About anything."

Quarnian searched for something to say. She pointed to the control panel. "Why wasn't that working when we first came in?"

"We were playing dead."

Quarnian nodded, suppressing the urge to look at her watch again. "I'd have thought there'd be a guard."

Sindona shrugged. "Can't waste anyone. You're important, but not that important. Besides, they don't know you have that suit."

"Frast, Rex's taking—"

Hurry up and get that thing on, Sindona suddenly thought at her. *They're bound to notice it's missing.*

"What? I thought you said not to—"

We can't waste time. Get it on and I'll try to find the alarm bypass.

But you—

Don't argue. They're probably right on our trail.

Quarnian understood just as another silent voice joined them.

There was something slimy about it from the very first thought. *Stop that, you two.*

A pair of crew members appeared in the corridor. Quarnian gave a shudder; one of them was Taril. She thought she could detect him smirking.

Return that.

Quarnian looked down; they were referring to the spacesuit in her hands. Trying not to smile, she did as she was asked.

We don't know where you've hidden the other one, but you can be sure you're not going to use it to escape. They focused their gaze on Sindona. *Come with us*.

"Where are you taking her?" Quarnian burst out.

Sindona looked at her. Her expression seemed to say, "It's OK."

It's not your concern, Taril thought. *Without your suit, you're harmless. But she is dangerous.*

He pointed a weapon at Sindona: a gray plastic tube a centimeter in diameter, about twice the length of her finger. Quarnian guessed it was the epilyzer.

Sindona pushed off to join them.

There was a knocking at the airlock door.

Quarnian's pulse began to pound along with it. *I want to know what will happen to her,* she projected as she tried to pretend the noise hadn't happened.

She will be dealt with.

More knocking.

What was that?

Quarnian tried to think. There was no point in denying it was there. But no plausible story came to mind. *I don't know.*

Taril pointed the epilzyer at her; she braced herself for another feeling of helplessness. *You don't know?*

I have no idea. Quarnian felt her thoughts being scrutinized for overtones she had no control over. She wished she could think of a better story.

Suddenly, Sindona pushed past them and grabbed the suit. "Here, Quarnian! Escape!" She moved her arms to toss it.

She stopped moving and began twitching. Sindona was suddenly in a fit; her body trembled, her eyes darted around. Out of her mouth came tortured grunts and squeaks.

The two men dragged her away. She was helpless and unresisting; spittle sprayed uncontrollably from her mouth.

Quarnian felt numb; she stared at the hallway they had dragged Sindona down. So that was what *she* had looked like. She was glad Rex or Bruce hadn't seen her that way.

Rex knocked again. She could sense his impatience; she opened the lock.

He came out looking angry. "What kept you so long? Where's Sindona?"

Quarnian told him. She didn't mention what she looked like when they took her away.

"Oh," Rex said, very softly.

There was no reason to rehash failure. "Is the ship all right?"

"I don't know. There was someone out there; I didn't want to chance them catching a glimpse of me. I got a quick check of supplies, though. Nothing seems to be missing."

Quarnian nodded. "Let's hope they leave it that way. I'd hate to escape here just to run out of food."

A thoughtful look covered Rex's face. "You know, I could swear those people I saw weren't wearing suits."

"They weren't." Quarnian told him about the spacebreathers. "Did you get to see anything else?"

"Only a quick glance. Things seem to be all right, but I can't be sure."

"Well, we're just going to have to assume it is. I don't think we can risk being caught here again."

"What's our next move?"

"We'll discuss it in your cabin." Quarnian glided to the empty storage locker she had noticed when they first boarded. "Stash the suit here."

Rex did as she asked. "I hope they don't look in here."

Quarnian nodded. "So do I."

"It looks like all we have to do is add air," Rex said when they reached the relative safety of his room.

Quarnian smiled despite herself. "You make it sound easy. Any ideas how to put it there?"

"I've been thinking about that. They must have some air tanks somewhere. Sindona can tell us . . ." He stopped. "I guess we're going to have to find out ourselves."

"For the moment." Quarnian felt an inner weariness roll over her; now they were down to two. In many ways, they were the two least equipped for the job. She closed her eyes.

There was too much pressure. And for what? It was hard to keep up hope; it wasn't likely they'd find what they needed. Even if they found air tanks, they'd have to get them to the *Wreckless*. The crew weren't idiots.

She felt a touch on her shoulder.

She lashed out reflexively, connecting with something even before her eyes opened again. A grunt exploded behind her.

Rex was doubled over, floating away from her. Evidently her blow had landed in his stomach.

"What's the idea?"

"Quarn," Rex gasped out. "Why'd you do that?" His breath slowly came back to him. "Frast, you can hit."

"What were you trying to do?"

"Don't get upset. I didn't mean anything."

"Just because I let you make love to me once, it doesn't mean—"

"Oh, can it. I wasn't trying anything."

"Then, why—?"

"Because you looked like you needed to be held." Rex's anger now matched her own.

She felt like her insides had collapsed. "Held?"

"Sure." Rex _had_ straightened now. "I think of other things besides sex, you know." He now seemed stiff as an iron rod as he pointed to the door. "Now, if you'll please go. . . ."

She started to turn, then stopped. "No, Rex. Look . . . I'm sorry. I'm very touchy right now."

Rex was silent, a cold look on his face.

"Rex, I . . ."

He looked away from her. "I'm not interested. Go find out about Sindona."

The words hurt. "Rex, please, I . . ." He showed no sign of paying attention, but she went on, impelled by something she couldn't name. "I . . . you were right. I need a hug." In other times she might have manipulated those words, aimed them like an arrow to get what she wanted. She realized that this time she meant them.

Rex said nothing for several endless moments. Then, slowly, he turned. His eyes seemed softer than usual as he stretched out his arms to her.

Chapter Seventeen

Quarnian had Rex search the ship; there was no danger he'd accidentally broadcast anything. He might be able to move around more easily than she could.

He was back in an hour.

"Nothing, Quarn," he said, his face telling her at once he wasn't bringing good news. "There's too much they're not letting me go near. If there are air tanks, they could be anywhere."

Quarnian nodded. She had thought of that before. "I guess it's up to me, then."

"What can you . . . ?"

"Find someone who'll tell us."

"But none of the crew will——"

"They might, if I ask the right questions. And the right people."

"Like who?"

She looked at him, hiding her annoyance. "I don't know. Maybe I'll just come out and ask if any auxiliary air tanks exist."

"And what if they don't?"

"Then we're stuck, aren't we?"

Rex nodded slowly.

There was an odd expression on his face. "All right," Quarnian said. "What's on your mind?"

"I didn't . . ."

"You picked the wrong person to try to fool."

Rex smiled slightly. "It's just that . . . well, five hundred years is a long time."

"And you think they don't have any air tanks."

"Not with anything in them."

She didn't say anything. Long shot on top of long shot. "You're still going through with this?"

She shrugged. "We don't have much choice, do we?"

Rex pushed himself nearer and took hold of her arms.

She struggled. "Rex, what are you—?"

"Look at me."

She didn't know why she obeyed him.

"Are we going to get out of here?" he demanded.

She couldn't turn away. Damn, she thought, I should have practiced my lying. "Sure we . . ."

But Rex had let go. "We're not."

She didn't feel the strength to deny it. She felt embarrassed, as though she had led him on for nothing. "Rex, I—"

"Don't say anything." Rex was silent as he thought. "Look, Quarn, your hunch is wrong. We're going to get out of here."

She nodded. "Right."

Rex stared at her, his expression stony. She hadn't a hint about what he was thinking. Then, suddenly, a tiny smile brightened his face. "This must be a record; I've got you to admit that three times."

His tone was a relief. "And you're the type to remind me of it."

"Quarn, let me tell you one thing. We're going to get out of here."

She nodded. "I suppose."

He shook his head. "No. You're sure. I think I know how you must feel."

The words brought a flare of anger; she controlled it. Everyone tried to figure out her feelings; no one had ever

come close. "You do?" she asked coolly, expecting another
fit of jealousy against her being a superwoman.

"I think so. I think you're so used to following your
hunches that you've come to think they're inevitable. Maybe
they are. But maybe what you feel about our getting out
isn't a hunch. Maybe it's just your pessimism about our
situation."

She smiled. "It's not exactly the best position to be in."

"No, it's not. But you're confusing your feelings with one
of your hunches."

Quarnian didn't answer. It was possible. Still, the discussion was meaningless if there weren't any air tanks.

She knew better than to say that. "You might be right."

Rex didn't answer immediately; he floated in front of her
like a judge. She felt uncomfortable.

"It must be hard to be a syron," he said.

The words struck home unerringly. Yes, it was hard,
damned hard. The syrons had a saying about it: The weight
of the pendant is greater than the weight of the stars. But
Rex was the first outsider to ever tell her he realized that.

"I've got to find out about that air," she said, her voice
only slightly choked. She swam toward the door.

"Where are you going?"

"To find Sindona." It was all she trusted herself to say.

The ship was beginning to remind Quarnian of a haunted
house. All it needed was cobwebs and footsteps echoing
through the corridors.

She guessed that Sindona was being held where they had
kept the two of them before. That wasn't much help. Quarnian had been too upset to take note of her passage there.
She'd just have to look around until she found it.

She wandered as best she could. Rex was right—they
were being careful where they let her go. Doors were locked;
white-haired people loomed menacingly to watch her as she
passed. If she took a wrong turn, they were quick to
intercept.

After two hours of this, she was exhausted. Moving in
zero gee took more energy than walking; she had to con-
stantly use muscles and motions that were still alien to her.

Even after all this time, she wasn't completely used to it. She wondered if she ever would be. . . .

No. She never would. She'd never have to.

She tried to relax. The thoughts of the crew itched in her brain; she was closer to them now. She decided that too much telepathy was a bad thing; if you had to keep overhearing thoughts, it was best to do it in moderation.

And suddenly, she realized how she could find Sindona.

She felt like kicking herself; weightlessness must have affected her brain. But mindspeech could cut through some of the walls. All she had to do was get close enough to pick up Sindona's thoughts.

Sindona, she thought as strongly as she could, *where are you?*

She tried to blank her mind to receive things better. All she could get was the random thoughts of others. *Sindona!* she tried again.

Then, very weakly, she heard her own name.

Sindona, I'm here, Quarnian thought. She visualized the corridor around her. *How do I get to you?*

And suddenly, she knew. It was like a forgotten memory dredged up from ages past. A map in her mind, "You are here" written on it with bright arrows. It was weak but understandable.

And there was something else, an overtone of emotion. Something about it frightened Quarnian. She rushed to get to Sindona.

Quarnian recognized the cells by their smell. "Sindona?" she asked, preferring sound to drive away the eeriness. "I want to know if—"

I can't answer, Quarnian.

The thought made her shudder, not in fear but in sympathy. It bloomed in her mind like an ancient dirge of infinite sadness. *What's wrong?*

They . . . they left me. They didn't reverse the epilyzer.

Quarnian remembered her own feeling of helplessness and shuddered again. *Aren't they going to . . . ?*

They're going to leave me this way. They—ouch. Banged my hand. I can't control it at all.

Quarnian put her eye to the peephole of the cell. There, bathed in the vomit-green light, Sindona was floating, quivering helplessly. Her face twitched in a thousand tics and grimaces; her eyes darted uncontrollably around the room.

Stop looking at me!

The thought was so strong it hurt. Quarnian looked away immediately. *I'm sorry. Is there anything . . . ?*

She stopped; it was a stupid question. She grabbed for the handle. With a little work, she might be able to break it open.

Her thought must have leaked out. *It won't work,* she felt Sindona project. *I'd still be . . . like this.*

Quarnian could sense her hysteria. *Calm down, Sindona.*

Calm down? You don't know what it's like!

I do, remember? It happened to me. Quarnian was beginning to feel upset along with her. *You've always been so confident. What happened to all that?*

Confident? Me? There was a strangled noise from inside the cell.

Quarnian went to look in, alarmed by the sound.

Stop! That was supposed to be a laugh. My confidence was an act.

Quarnian felt her stomach tighten once again. *What do you mean?*

I don't really think we're going to get out of here.

*But you always said . . . *

I hoped.

*You seemed so . . . *

I'm a lot better at hiding my feelings than you are. It's my naturally cheery disposition that fooled you.

Quarnian tried to think for herself. She might as well give up now; no one really thought they'd escape. Her ultimate mission might be to crew the *Staroamer*.

There's no way out, Sindona continued. *I've always known that. I just didn't dare let you know I knew. It gave me a little hope. A fool's hope.*

Nonsense. Quarnian hoped her pessimistic thoughts didn't leak through. *All we have to do is . . . *

* . . . is put air in the *Wreckless*. But there's no air to spare. And no way of getting it aboard. No tanks, no anything. We used up our reserves centuries ago; only recycling keeps us going. Any tanks we once had have been broken down for patches and repairs.*

"We'll get the air somehow," Quarnian mumbled.

How? By magic?

On that bitter note, the thoughts stopped, to be replaced with a general air of despair. Quarnian felt caught up in it; she fought against the tide. Her hand unconsciously closed around her pendant; it gave her an answer. "Sindona," she said out loud to ritualize the words, "I swear by the star to get you off the *Staroamer*."

So what? came the reply.

Quarnian explained what her oath meant.

There was an overtone of surprise in Sindona's answering thought. *You can't really mean that.*

Sindona, I—

Quarnian.

The thought was neither hers nor Sindona's. Quarnian looked up.

Taril grinned at her. *The captain wants to talk with you.*

His grin gave her a new resolve. She was going to get out of here or kill the smirking man.

You'll feel different when we spray you. He pulled out the epilyzer. *Are you going to come along?*

She did. She'd have to deal with him later.

Vorst greeted Quarnian with a smile that reminded her of a cat that had cornered a mouse. He was holding a drinking bulb in his left hand; Quarnian shook her head when he indicated another beside him.

Quarnian, he thought at her, *I wish you'd stop trying to get out of here.*

"You really think I will?"

Vorst laughed, the breath drawing inward like a rattle. "Let's use words then, if you're more comfortable with them. It's interesting using them—I've been getting lessons from your friend Bruce."

"Glad to hear he's such a help to you."

Vorst paid no attention to her sarcasm. "Bruce is quite intelligent. You should be so . . . No, never mind."

"I want out."

Vorst shook his head. "I'm afraid that's impossible. I think you should consider our point of view. We need people to help us."

"And to breed for you." Quarnian tried to keep rein on her anger; it didn't work.

"Yes," Vorst said. His voice had lost its hard edge. "I know how much you dislike the idea."

"Dislike isn't the word."

"I'm sorry, but everyone must pull his own weight around here. You certainly must be able to see that we can't allow it any way else. If you prefer, I can give you some leeway as to who you mate with. You could choose Rex, for example; he's well within acceptable norms."

Quarnian suppressed a shudder. "I don't want Rex. I don't want anyone." She looked at him suspiciously. "Why are you suddenly being so thoughtful?"

"You probably know why; it's because I think it'll be more effective."

"More than your pheromones?"

Vorst seemed embarrassed. "I *am* sorry about that. We just thought it would make things easier. If you prefer to mate without them . . ."

"Let's get one thing straight: I don't plan to mate at all."

"Then we will continue to use them," Vorst snapped. "If you want to be difficult, I'm quite willing to get tough with you."

Quarnian didn't say anything.

"I'd much rather have your cooperation," Vorst went on. "We'd like to find out about what a syron is."

Quarnian felt a chill of fear. "A syron? What do you mean?"

Evidently her voice wasn't as innocent as she tried to make it. "We know about it. You've been broadcasting most of your thoughts to us."

"That was in the beginning," Quarnian mumbled, too numbed to become any more depressed.

"You're still doing it. Sindona's lessons haven't helped you."

Her depression had turned into despair. She tried to summon up the strength to rebound again; all she was able to do was stare at Vorst.

She hated the fat, pasty face, the empty blue eyes, all complacent in its superiority. Her life would be spent hating it. And, like all hates, it would do her no good.

Then suddenly, a thought came to her. It was her own, the type of thought she hadn't had in ages: a hunch.

Vorst was lying. The lessons *had* helped.

It was a minor victory, but it gave her back her spine. She knew she was probably still slipping occasionally, most likely when her emotions overcame her practicing. But if she kept an eye on that, she'd be all right.

"Why don't you just accept things, like Bruce has? He's been very helpful in the hydroponics."

"Because I can't. Because I'm not . . ." She stopped; she had to try to make him listen to reason again. "But why bother with me? I'm going to give you nothing but trouble. There are plenty of people to choose from on New Wichatah. Probably some like Bruce who'd love to join you."

Vorst smiled. "We want you; you're unique. Besides, what would we get? Certainly not the best the planet has to offer."

"How do you know?"

Vorst shrugged. "We went over this before. I'm not interested in the others; only you."

Quarnian knew enough to give up. "What about Sindona? Are you going to let her out?"

"Eventually."

"At least let her have control of herself."

"Eventually. When there's no danger of you escaping. Without her help, you'll never get out of here."

"But it's such a waste. . . . "

The captain's eyes narrowed. "We don't waste anything on the *Staroamer*," he said, coldly furious. "Nothing. Ever. If you do escape, it will be because of Sindona. We're going to make sure that doesn't happen."

Quarnian barely heard the last sentence. Her mind was churning. She suddenly knew that there was a way out. Their biggest problem could be solved and she realized how she might solve it.

Vorst's burst of anger was over. "I think that's enough for both of us. Thank you for helping me with my language."

Quarnian thanked him back. She meant it.

Quarnian went straight to the archive room. For the first time in ages, the lack of gravity made her think she was flying. Not that she paid much attention; she was too busy going over things in her mind.

The terminal refused to tell her what she asked it. She took that for a good sign. She tried more roundabout ways and slowly began to pick up morsels of information, identifying them by their absence. Nothing direct, of course, but enough to make her feel more and more confident.

"Well?"

She started at the sound of Rex's voice. "Well, what?" she mumbled as she pushed another button.

"Are there any air tanks?"

"Air tanks? No." Another dead end on the screen. Good, she *was* on the right track. Now, if she could only . . .

"Sindona said there weren't any?"

"Right." She frowned at the data on the display. Not what she had expected. But, wait, she had forgotten . . .

She felt herself being spun around.

She had never seen Rex so upset. "Damn it, stop fiddling with that. You're going to have plenty of time. We're stuck here, aren't we?"

Her mind suddenly returned to the room. She began to laugh. "I'm sorry, Rex. No, we're not stuck here. We're going to get out."

"Without air? You're crazy."

She shook her head. "With air. Without air tanks."

"You *are* crazy."

"No, wait, listen to me. I felt the same when Sindona told me. If I hadn't talked with the captain, I might have given up."

"The captain? What did he say?"

"He told me that nothing on the *Staroamer* was ever wasted. Tell me, what's the most vital element for a spaceship to have?"

"Air," Rex said instantly. "But what does that—?"

Quarnian nodded. "Air. Tell me, do you really think they'd let all the air in the *Wreckless* float out into space?"

Rex was silent; she could almost hear his mind clicking. "But without tanks . . ."

"So they found some other way. We know their science is more advanced than ours. Since air is so vital, they've probably spent a lot of time researching it. It only makes sense that they've found new methods of storage."

Rex whistled. "So you were thinking the archive might tell you what."

Quarnian shook her head. "I know it wouldn't; which means I'm on the right track. I think they've perfected some chemical form of storage."

"But what about Sindona? She must have known."

"Why would she? It's out of her field. But I suspect we'll find what we're looking for in that lab she showed me."

Rex slowly nodded. "Sounds possible. But how do you . . . ?" He stopped and grinned. "Don't tell me. Another hunch."

Quarnian smiled back. "I hadn't thought of it, but I suppose it is."

"You haven't had too many lately."

"You're right. I'm not sure why." Her smile grew wider. "I'm beginning to get another one, too. Let's hope it's a good sign."

"What is it?"

She motioned him closer and playfully kissed his cheek. He was sweet; he deserved it. "I think," she whispered, as though speaking too loud would make it untrue, "I think we're going to get out of here."

Chapter Eighteen

"I'm going alone," Quarnian said in a tone that plainly meant it was the end of the argument.

Rex ignored it. "You'll need me. How will you get past the lock?"

"You think I'd have gotten anything accomplished if locks stopped me? Don't worry, I'll be all right." She pushed off for the door.

"If you go alone," Rex said coldly, "I'll sabotage you."

Quarnian looked at him and sighed. They had been discussing the matter way too long. It was no trick to read his face; the anger on it was as false as a steel flower. "You know you don't mean that."

"I do."

She wondered just what he was trying to prove. He hadn't been near the lab, and now he wanted to go along with her. It would be hard enough for her to keep out of sight; the two of them would get nowhere. She would just have to call his bluff.

But she hesitated. Maybe it wasn't fair to always be right about him. Too embarrassing; his ego would have to be protected if things were to go smoothly. "All right," she said. "Follow me."

They moved through the corridors slowly, pushing off the bulkheads as silently as they could manage. Each intersection or door was a challenge: a quick look to see if anyone was there, a leap across it if there wasn't, a slow, cautious glide if they suspected there was.

Quarnian took it easy, trying to locate landmarks. One trip was hardly enough to remember anything, but her practice in finding her way around was a help.

The corridors were quiet. Quarnian had chosen to go during the crew's sleep period; there were fewer people about and the lab would probably be empty.

The first sign of a snag appeared as they reached another cross corridor.

Quarnian poked her head out to scout. She saw something.

Too much: she recognized Taril.

She pushed back. He had been looking in her direction. She couldn't be sure if he had seen her.

"Is something . . . ?" Rex whispered.

She shushed him with a glare. She had to assume Taril hadn't gotten a good look at her; if he had, it didn't matter what they did. Grabbing Rex's hand, she leaped for the nearest door.

With her adrenaline flowing, she reached for the handle, praying it wasn't locked.

It didn't move.

It took all her effort to keep from panicking. Quickly, she pushed for another door across the hall, Rex struggling to keep up with her.

It wouldn't budge, either.

She knew she didn't have time to get past the lock. Taril should have been there by now; she didn't dare try to listen to what he was thinking. It was hard enough keeping her emotions under control so she wouldn't project.

A third door beckoned, the only chance. She tried it.

This time, it opened. She pulled Rex inside.

Her heart racing, she tried to pick up Taril's thoughts.

I tell you I saw her, she received.

Another thought glided out at her, rich with amusement. *You have her on your mind too much, Taril. But, all right, take a look. But if Vorst finds out you've left your guard station, you're taking all the blame.*

Quarnian felt the coolness of relief. All they had to do was lie low until . . .

"Quarnian, where are we?"

She turned to Rex and noticed their surroundings for the first time. The cabin was not bare. It was filled with signs of habitation: a sleepnet, clothing attached to the wall, dirty underwear that floated like a jellyfish in the corner. "I don't know," she said, "but I hope the resident doesn't come back."

She went back to the door to see if she could hear Taril outside.

See, she heard in her mind, *no one.*

She could tell Taril was unconvinced. *All right, you win the bet. Let me go and get it from my cabin.*

Quarnian felt a chill. No, it couldn't be . . . "Rex, hide," she hissed.

"Hide? Where? What for?"

She pointed toward a storage locker that looked big enough to hold him. "Hurry!"

Rex knew better than to argue now; her tone was too urgent. He disappeared just as the door to the cabin opened.

Taril grinned as soon as he saw her; she didn't like the looks of it. *I thought I saw you.* His face quickly became a frown. *What are you doing here?*

Quarnian wasn't sure what to tell him. "Guess," she said, speaking to give Rex some idea what was going on.

Taril looked at her. *I guess you saw me and tried to hide in here. Am I right?*

"Not even close."

She could tell Taril didn't believe her. *Then what is it?*

What indeed? "I . . . I wanted to apologize."

Taril asked her for what; it gave her time to plan her words.

"I know I can't get out of here. I've accepted the inevitable." She switched to mindspeech; Rex shouldn't have to hear what she was going to have to say. *We are to be mated, so we might as well become friends.*

Taril's grin returned, wider than ever. She could almost feel the lust in his thoughts. *I'm glad you've seen reason.*

Sure. When the time comes, I'll be willing.

We don't have to wait until then, Taril thought.

Quarnian fought to hide her revulsion. *But I'm not ready. . . . *

He thought question marks as her; she'd have to do better than that.

I mean—

We don't have to make children, you realize.

No, Quarnian thought, *I didn't. I thought that you—*

We're still human. Pleasure is very important to us. He moved nearer, smiling. *I like the color of your hair. The brown makes you look . . . interesting.*

She somehow managed to control her instinct to retreat. She hated him, everything about him. She would have gladly chopped holes in his heart.

She fought her feelings. If he guessed her real thoughts . . .

Taril! What's keeping you?

Taril stopped. *Damn, I'm on duty. I can't leave now.*

Who was that?

No one, Borix.

Are you trying to get out of our bet?

Never. Taril looked at Quarnian. *I have to go now. I'll be off duty in two hours. Wait for me.*

Quarnian agreed. Two hours were two hours; she could get a lot accomplished in that time.

Taril reached into a cupboard and pulled out a brown plastic bottle. It gurgled as he went out the door.

Quarnian released a gallon of air from her lungs. "It's all right," she said to Rex, keeping her voice low. "You can come out now."

Rex appeared slowly, as though he expected a trick. "How'd you get him to go? And why'd you suddenly stop talking with him?"

"Later," Quarnian said. "We've got to get moving."

"Wait a minute. I want to show you something."

"What is it?"

"It's something I found in the locker."

"Damn it, stop trying to be mysterious. What is it?"

"This." He reached into his pocket and pulled out a gray shaft on a handle: an epilyzer. "I think it might be a weapon."

"It sure is. The one I told you about. Now put it back. Taril's bound to realize it's gone."

Rex shook his head. "I don't think so. There must be a dozen of them in there. He'll never miss just one."

A regular arsenal, Quarnian thought. "All right, let's go. We don't have much time."

The corridor was empty when they looked out. Quarnian put her mouth to Rex's ear. "You'll have to look," she whispered so softly she could barely hear it herself. "See if they're looking this way."

Rex took a careful peek, then quickly beckoned her by.

They were lucky the rest of the way: no one in sight. Quarnian stopped in front of a vaguely familiar door. "This is it," she whispered.

"Are you sure?"

"Please don't ask me that, Rex."

Rex smiled.

Quarnian listened with her ears and her mind; there was no sound of life inside. The door was locked, but the lock was flimsy; obviously they trusted each other aboard ship. Quarnian was able to jiggle with it until it clicked open. "All right," she said once they were safely inside. "Let's start looking."

They went through the room systematically. The lab was cluttered with floating glassware and electronics; its cabinets held chemicals and supplies. A few of the devices were new to Quarnian, but they just didn't feel like what they were looking for. The rest were variations on what any research lab might have.

"It's no use," Rex said. "I can't tell one thing from another."

Quarnian agreed. "We're going to have to find their notes."

"I don't see any . . ."

"Of course not," Quarnian snapped. She was becoming acutely conscious of the passage of time. If Taril didn't find her in his cabin, he'd know she had lied. She pointed to the computer terminal. "They're in there. I think this one will be willing to tell us what Sindona's won't."

Rex looked annoyed. "Why didn't you look there in the first place?"

She looked at him coldly. "Because I could be wrong. Because the computer might need an access code—one that I'd never guess. Because it's hooked into the same circuit as the archive terminal—and programmed to keep its mouth shut. Are those enough reasons for you?"

Rex was silent for several seconds. "You must think I'm an idiot," he mumbled.

"No," she said, her annoyance spent. "You're not used to thinking this way. Why, when I was on Radis, I had to . . ." She stopped. "We can reminisce later."

She went over to the computer. "Well," she said, taking a deep breath, "here goes."

She flicked the power switch; the screen glowed green.

"*Enter name and ID number*," it said.

"We're stuck," Rex said.

"Ssssh." Her name was out of the question. How about Sindona's? Quarnian knew her ID from working with her before. She'd have to risk it.

She explained her plan to Rex. "If anything goes wrong, I want you out the door. Get back to your cabin. I'll try to get the information to you." She tried to make her voice confident; she had a feeling that Vorst would never let her have the chance.

"Quarn, I—"

"Do as I say!" She smiled. "Sorry to shout, but you're a lousy soldier. Every time I give an order, I get an argument."

"If you didn't order me . . ."

"Rex, please. Save it for later. Go to the door."

Rex grudgingly did as she asked.

Quarnian took another deep breath and looked at the keyboard. "Here goes," she whispered. She typed the letters: *S-I-N-D-O-N-A 1-4-9-2.*

The screen went blank.

It's all right, she told herself. Standard procedure, that's all.

The screen lit again. "*Question?*" it said.

Quarnian let her breath out. No alarms, at least.

See? I told you I heard something.

A hand touched her shoulder just as the thought came clear. She jumped and was barely able to suppress a shriek.

"Quarn," Rex whispered near her ear, "there's someone outside. I heard ..."

"I know," she hissed. "I'm picking them up. Quiet."

It's probably Addra, came the thought from outside. *You know how she gets involved in problems.*

I don't know. It may be the new ones.

They would never have gotten past Taril and Borix.

You know those two. They couldn't see an airbreather if he blew in their faces. I'd like to check.

Addra? You in there?

Quarnian froze her thoughts. Blank, blank—give them nothing.

Nothing.

Then let's open the door and check.

There was the sound of a key scraping against the lock. No time to hide; their only chance was a bluff.

Who is it? Quarnian thought, making the idea as annoyed as she could.

Addra? Is that you?

Who do you think it is? Quarnian let the anger color her thoughts; it might help to disguise them. *Leave me alone. I'm busy.*

*You sound strange. . . . *

Damn it, go away!

Quarnian could sense a hesitation in their thoughts; she did all she could to keep from letting anything slip.

We're sorry, Addra.

She could feel the two men leaving.

Quarnian allowed herself to relax.

"Are we all right?" Rex asked.

She nodded. "They're gone."

"What happened?"

Quarnian shook her head and smiled. "Someday I'm going to have to tell you about these conversations. Let's just say I convinced them I was someone else." She turned to the computer. "Let's start looking."

It would have helped if she had known what she was looking for. A lot of discoveries had been made during the voyage: the epilyzer, their clothes, new drugs, new plants, special fertilizers. From the look of things, pure science had become their major form of recreation. She looked through the files as carefully as she could, trying to repress the urge to keep checking her watch.

Then, as her search led her to chemistry, she found it. As soon as she saw the information on the screen, she whistled. "Look at that, will you?"

Rex squinted. "Is it metal?"

"More like a plastic. Airstone, they call it. Combines with oxygen in the presence of heat. Sprinkle carbon on it and it gives it off."

"How big a rock would they need for the *Wreckless*?"

"Probably about half a meter in diameter." She shook her head. "This *is* something."

"Very convenient," Rex agreed. "Where do they keep the stuff?"

"I'm looking. Place of storage: hold twenty-three B. Well, that's our answer. Wherever that is."

Rex smiled. "I think I know."

She looked at him. Was he joking? "Where?"

"Where those guards were."

Quarnian didn't answer.

"Why else would they be guarding it like that? If they're keeping an eye on something around here, it's because of us."

"Rex," Quarnian said, "I believe you're right." She glanced at her watch; they had been there nearly an hour and a half. She flicked off the power on the computer. "We've got to be going. You go back to our section. I'll be there later."

Rex frowned. "Where are you going?"

She hadn't had time to make up a good lie. "To . . . to see Sindona."

He shook his head. "What's the real story?"

She sighed and explained her promise to Taril.

Rex was shocked. "Why? Just come back with me; you can tell him you changed your mind. There's no need—"

"There is." Quarnian felt drained. "Don't you think I would if I could? If I'm not there waiting for Taril, he'll know I lied to him. He'll be suspicious, and even the hint of suspicion will sink us."

"But he's going to want to—"

"I know," Quarnian said bitterly. "It can't be helped."

Rex ignored her tone. "No," he said, "it *can* be helped. You don't have to show up there."

Quarnian's mouth was dry. "I'm sorry, Rex. I have to."

He stared at her, his mouth a red line. "I think you *want* to make love with him."

"Don't be . . ." She couldn't finish; the liquid that should have been in her mouth was filling her eyes. She knew she couldn't make herself sound angry. "Rex, I have to. I have no choice in the matter. It's . . . one of my hunches." She breathed quickly, tottering on the edge of losing her self-control. "Damn," she mumbled, wiping her eyes.

"Quarn?"

She tried to see his face through the tears. "I hate looking emotional, and I hate every time this happens to me."

"It's happened before?"

Quarnian wanted to force a laugh; she couldn't. "You think I'm a virgin? I follow my intuition. I've made love to eight people I detested, just to do things it told me to do. And I hated it. Hated it, hated it, hate—"

He was holding his hand over her mouth. "All right. You made your point. Quiet down or someone'll hear you."

She took several deep breaths as she felt a tear float off her face. "Frast, it's a nightmare." She sniffled and looked into his face. "I'm sorry, Rex. There's no other way."

Rex grunted. "All right, Quarn. If you have to, you have to." The words were grudging.

"That's why that pheromone business scared me like it did. It was like those other times—only worse. At least in the past I knew I was doing it for a reason. It was only a small consolation, but it gave me a chance to save some self-respect. With that spray, I didn't even have that."

"I understand," Rex said.

She knew from his tone that he didn't, but she was not going to comment on it. She felt a little better now.

"I guess we'd better be going."

Quarnian nodded. Silently, they left the lab.

Chapter Nineteen

Quarnian felt numb and tired, and somewhat unclean when she finally returned to her own cabin. It was not as bad as she had expected, as long as she pretended that Taril was someone else.

She wanted nothing more than to sleep, but a knock on the door prevented that.

Rex came in. "How . . . ?"

"Please," Quarnian said, holding up a hand. "No questions. I don't want to think about it."

"I've been thinking myself."

Quarnian didn't like the way he said it. "Yes?"

"We can go into that hold tonight." He held up the epilyzer. "I'll just use this on the guards and—"

"Sorry, Rex. No."

"Why not? You think you're the only one around here who can plan anything? You planned that last expedition; look where it got you."

It was as though he had kicked her; it was a hard fight to keep her hurt secret. "Rex, I told you—"

"You could have found a way out."

"Dammit, Rex, I had no choice!"

"You were very convincing," Rex nodded. "But that's your job. To fool mere humans like me."

Quarnian fought to remain calm. "Rex, you're talking nonsense. How in the planets—"

"I had a lot of time to think while you were with him. I say we get out now. If he's nothing to you, then you'll go along with me."

A ridiculous suspicion crossed Quarnian's mind. "Are you jealous of him?"

"No," Rex said.

Quarnian knew he was lying. She waited.

"All right, I am. You won't even let me near you, but you let him do whatever he wants just because of some flimsy promise I didn't even hear."

"Rex," Quarnian said, very quietly, "are you in love with me?"

Rex didn't answer.

Quarnian sighed. It had happened too many times before; she should have expected it. "Now let's get one thing straight. You're a friend. I don't love you, I don't love Taril, I don't love anyone. I can't afford to, not with what I have to go through. I'm sorry, Rex, but that's just the way things have to be."

Rex couldn't meet her eyes. "Then why *are* you waiting here? Why don't you like my plan?"

"It's not a bad plan. It's just . . . Well, take the epilyzer. It'll stop the guard, all right, but it won't stop them from calling for help. They don't need voices for that. So we'll have to hit everyone on the ship. Even if we managed that— and we can't—we'd have to figure out what to do with everyone. We can't leave them that way; they'll never come out of it."

"Leave them," Rex grumbled; it was only a token argument. "They deserve it."

"No, they don't, and you know it. Besides, I need time. They may be suspicious of us right now; I can't be sure I didn't project to Taril. We may have to wait until they're not keeping such a close eye on us. And we have to get Sindona out somehow."

"Do we? I mean, she's been great to us, but if she's going to slow us up—"

"I promised her. It will be all of us or none at all."

"Probably none," Rex grumbled.

"Quite possibly. Look, Rex, we'll argue this later. I'm beat; I've had too much to handle today. Why don't you try to find my spacesuit? Just give me a chance to rest right now; I think I'm entitled to that."

Rex nodded and left the room; Quarnian collapsed into her sleepnet and began a fitful sleep.

It seemed that Quarnian had just shut her eyes when someone knocked on her door again; only the sour taste in her mouth told her she had slept at all. "Rex, please," she mumbled as she blinked her gritty eyes, "come back later. I'm tired."

I have come to get you.

The thought in her head startled her awake. The mind was unfamiliar to her, and she didn't like the way the words were sent to her. *Go away.*

Quarnian heard the door swing open; she shook her head slowly. "What now?" she asked, looking up at her visitor.

It was a woman, a member of the crew that Quarnian hadn't seen before. Her hair had the slightest tinge of blond interrupting the whiteness, crowning an oblong face with a short but thin nose. *I am Rixalt,* she thought. *You are to be put to work.*

Quarnian began to unzip her sleepnet; she knew there was no point in resisting. *So soon? I didn't think you'd trust me to do anything.*

Taril has vouched for you.

I'll bet he has, Quarnian thought to herself. *Where am I going to be working?*

Follow me.

Quarnian did, wondering how this new development would affect their escape. It certainly wouldn't help. They had been lucky so far; they had been left alone. There had been no reason to watch them, to take people from more important tasks; there was no place they could go, anyway.

Now, however, she wouldn't have the time that she had

had before; everything would have to be rushed or left up to Rex. She didn't quite trust him.

Rixalt led her into an unfamiliar section of the ship. The corridors were cleaner, less musty; this must be where the crew spent most of their time. Quarnian could pick out nearby minds buzzing around her.

And then she felt a sudden inarticulate feeling of misery being projected into her mind. It was strong, as though several people were being starved and tortured at once. Yet, somehow, she had the feeling that assistance wasn't needed. She tried to puzzle it out.

Then she heard the sound of the crying.

She smiled despite herself. Babies. The next generation.

Rixalt glanced at her for a second, then, with a gentle smile, led her to a door. She pushed it open.

The children ranged from infants to about age six. Some of the smaller ones were crying; a woman floated among them, passing out formula.

The older ones were playing; Quarnian recognized it as a form of tag. They darted around the cabin, laughing and squealing, flying through the space like butterflies.

Whatever they had evolved into, they still acted like children; the ship was a vast playground to fly in and invent games in.

Quarnian's smile grew.

You like them?

Quarnian looked at Rixalt. *Is this going to be my job?* Her emotions were mixed. It would remind her too much of what they wanted her for.

Rixalt shook her head. *I thought you might like to see them. I can feel what you think about us. I wanted you to know we're still much like you.*

"I see," Quarnian whispered. She decided she liked Rixalt. She followed her back into the corridor.

Be careful going in, Rixalt warned.

The door, as usual, was unlabeled. Quarnian wondered what she should be careful of. Shrugging, she pulled open the door and floated in.

And crashed to the floor.

The sudden change to gravity had taken her by surprise. She got up slowly, rubbing a sore elbow. The gravity seemed weaker than Earth-normal, but it had been so long she couldn't be sure.

A hand helped her get on her feet. "I thought Rixalt warned you," Addra said.

"Not well enough. And I'm surprised you're speaking aloud."

Addra smiled. "I thought you might like to feel more at home. I practice a lot with your friend."

"Bruce?" It seemed ages since Quarnian had had word of him. "How is he?"

"Just fine. He's beginning to act like a born crewman. I wish we could teach him to mindspeak, but he's still been very helpful. I hope you're going to be as cooperative as he is."

"I am," Quarnian said. "But I'm curious—why do you have this artificial gravity in here?"

Addra pointed to several bottles stacked neatly in a cabinet on the wall. "It's a lot easier dealing with liquids if they're not floating off."

Quarnian didn't bother to ask why they hadn't put gravity elsewhere; it certainly used up precious energy. "So you want me to help you in here?"

Addra laughed; it sound like a hoarse croak mixed with music. "Not yet. We don't quite trust you *that* far. There's always a chance this is a trick. Although, after what Taril said . . ."

Quarnian felt herself turning red. Had that overgrown stud horse told everyone on the ship about them? Immediately, she knew she had projected the thought; she sent out other thoughts concerning lack of privacy to cover.

"It's all right," Addra said. "I'm sorry I said it. I realize you prize privacy more highly than we do. But I guess what happens between you and Taril isn't really my business."

"Or anyone's," Quarnian said.

Addra nodded. "Or anyone's. Taril can be a bit of a . . . a . . ."

"A boor."

"That's the word. A boor. Now, about your job . . ."

Addra walked over to a gleaming white cupboard and took out a bottle of pale silver liquid, translucent as mica. Attached to its top was a large sponge. "I'm afraid it's not very glamorous. The ship is made mostly of steel. As you can probably guess, rust is a problem."

Quarnian nodded. "Weakens the structure."

"Well, yes, but more importantly, it uses up oxygen. Iron oxide, you know. And we can't waste that. We don't have a ready supply."

Quarnian grunted, keeping her thoughts about the oxygen from the *Wreckless* to herself.

"This chemical frees the oxygen from the rust. Just rub it on; a thin coat is plenty. It takes a few hours before you'd notice any changes, so don't worry about that. You can start in the hydroponics; it's always a problem there. Too much moisture."

Quarnian took the bottle; the sponge appeared to be moistened through a hole in the cap; a squeeze would saturate it even under zero gee.

"Any questions?"

Quarnian had none. The job could be a golden opportunity; she could see more of the ship, maybe even find the missing spacesuit. As soon as she had the chance, she'd ask Sindona where it was. She hoped they hadn't moved it.

There was a lot of rust in the hydroponics, once you looked for it. Quarnian wondered if the bottle would last more than a few minutes. She discovered it did; even though it looked as though it held less than a liter, the amount of liquid had barely shrunk after half an hour of diligent daubing. Either the sponge emitted only a molecule-thick layer of liquid or the bottle was somehow larger inside than out. She was trying to decide when she heard a voice behind her.

"Lady? That you?"

Bruce was smiling broadly.

"How are you, Bruce? Are you the one watching me?"

He shrugged. "We all do. Take turns."

Quarnian understood. "What are you doing these days?"

"The plants," Bruce said, gesturing at the garden. "I tend them."

There was an almost childish pride in the way he spoke the last three words. Quarnian smiled. She doubted that Bruce had ever seen much more than scraggly weeds pushing up between cracked pavement before he left New Wichatah. Now he was a farmer; the change had done him wonders.

"Must go," he mumbled. "Break's over."

Quarnian watched him as he went over to a yellow-stemmed plant. He began to fuss over it like a nearcat over her kittens. Well, at least someone's happy here, she thought. If they didn't get out, if her hunch turned out to be wrong or not a hunch at all, that might be something to grasp on to.

She returned to her task, thinking of escape plans as she treated the rust.

"Where were you, Quarn?" Rex asked. "I've been trying to find you for hours."

She told him. He seemed slightly skeptical, as though he had other ideas, but didn't say anything. "Any luck finding the suit?"

"None. I have a suspicion where, though."

"Where?"

"The same place they're keeping our air."

Quarnian considered the idea. "Perhaps, but . . ."

"But what?"

"Well, Sindona removed two suits already. I doubt if the guards would have let her do it."

"Don't you ever get tired of being right?" Rex snapped.

She decided to ignore his annoyance; who knew what charges another confrontation would bring. "All right, Rex. That's enough. I'll talk to Sindona. She can tell us."

"I've been thinking about her, too. We've only got two spacesuits. Even if we got Bruce's, it'd never fit her. How is she going to get onto the *Wreckless*?"

Quarnian hadn't considered that; she hadn't had the time. "I don't know. Maybe she's a spacebreather." She knew that it sounded like a weak stab in the dark.

"Well, wonder of wonders. You don't know something."

Quarnian didn't comment. His jealousy was getting

annoying. Some men have no idea how to behave when they're in love. They go too far, one way or another, especially those who aren't used to showing their feelings. You really need practice to understand the fine art of making a fool of yourself over someone else.

She wished she could put an end to the friction; it wasn't doing either of them any good.

And she realized she was being foolish. There was an answer: she could pretend to love him back. She could easily do it; it wasn't as repugnant to her as pretending to Taril, and it would certainly be better than this constant undertone of tension.

She'd have to start slowly. "Rex, I wish you'd drop this chip from your shoulder. I do like you; I don't see why you have to be mad at me."

Rex grunted.

"We're friends. We have to stick together. I'm sorry if you—"

"That's enough, Quarn."

"Rex, I just wanted you to know—"

"Stop playing with me!"

The shout made the ensuing silence seem deafening. Quarnian felt warmth glow in her cheeks. Rex glared at her.

"I'm sorry," she said, very softly. "I really don't like having to manipulate you."

"Why? Am I any different from the others you've treated like pawns? You're so used to it you can't help yourself. You don't give a frast about anyone."

Every word was a hammer blow; a syron couldn't have been more on target. Quarnian fought to keep control of her emotions. Even if she showed her hurt, Rex would think it was a trick. "Rex," she said, her voice strange and uncertain. "I *am* sorry. Really. I don't want you to be upset at me. We have to work together. And—I know you're not going to believe this, but I'm going to say it anyway—we *are* friends, no matter what I was trying to do. Surely you know that's true."

"Yeah," Rex said. "I know that." His voice hinted strongly at sarcasm.

"Please, Rex . . ." She realized there was no point in

saying anything more. "I'll go talk with Sindona," she mumbled and left the room.

By now she didn't need a guide to find the cells, and it was a good thing, too; she just couldn't seem to pick up Sindona's thoughts.

Sindona? she projected when she got there.

Quarnian waited for an answer. All that came into her mind were vague hints of silent conversation from others.

She felt nervous. Had they moved her somewhere else? *Sindona?*

Then, faint and weak, she heard an answer. *My name,* came the thought. *I know that's my name.*

The overtones in the thought scared Quarnian. *Sindona, it's Quarnian. Are you all right?*

All right, all right, all right, allright—

"Sindona!" Quarnian shouted.

The answering thought was soft and dreamy. *Hello, Quarnian. Are you really there? It's so hard to tell.*

I'm here. What have they done to you?

Nothing. A dismal-tinged cheer colored the thought. *They've left me alone. I'm only going insane. Nothing to worry about.*

*No, you're not . . . *

Don't argue with me. You're just another figment of my imagination.

Quarnian felt a chill. "You're wrong, Sindona," she said. "I'm real. Listen to me."

Real?

"Listen. You're all right. I've got good news. We've found air for the *Wreckless*." She explained about the airstone.

The giddiness in Sindona's thoughts decreased. *Then we can get out.*

Yes, very soon. Be patient.

Patient! The thought was bitter. *I can't do anything but quiver. I've been lying here all these weeks with nothing to do but think and dream. I can't tell one from another anymore.*

All these weeks? Sindona, you've only been here a few days. I talked with you the day before yesterday.

Seems like weeks. Her thoughts took on the dreamy quality again.

Get control of yourself, Sindona. You can't be going crazy.

Why not? Crazy people don't have to think. They can live in dreams. Dreams are so much better than life, don't you think?

Sindona!

Her thoughts had turned dark. *I'll never escape from here. Better to be crazy. I'll spend the rest of my life in this goddamned ship.*

Sindona, listen to me. We're going to get you out of here. We're nearly ready. We're going to escape.

What difference does it make? I'll still be . . . like this.

Quarnian fought against the sorrow Sindona projected. *We've got an epilyzer. We can put you back to normal.*

Ah, just what I wanted to hear! A beautiful story. And the handsome prince will come along and I'll live happily ever after. See—I do know Earth legends. I'm an archivist.

Sindona, read my thoughts. You know how to tell if I'm lying. We have an epilyzer.

It took a few seconds for Sindona to answer. *It's true,* came her thought, weak and wondering.

If you want, we could fix you up right now.

That would be . . . No, you can't. They'd know who did it.

Quarnian had thought of that also; Sindona's words were a hopeful sign. She still had her wits. *It might take a few more days before we're ready. Are you sure you can hold out?*

No. But I'll try . . . I think I'll be all right once I have control of myself.

Quarnian nodded. She hoped so. Probably there was some sort of treatment aboard ship if she did go crazy; the captain would not have let her get this way otherwise. But it was doubtful anyone on New Wichatah could deal with her as easily. If Sindona did lose her sanity, the kindest thing might be to leave her here.

Quarnian put that thought out of her mind; she had sworn by the star. She explained the reason for her visit.

*I found the spacesuits in . . . * Sindona thought, and Quarnian saw the location in her mind; it was a storage space just off the hydroponics. *I doubt if they've moved the one I left. But they'll never let you in there.*

*You let me worry about that. I've got to go now. Just remember: we *are* going to get you out of here.*

You are.

It wasn't until Quarnian was halfway back to her cabin that she realized she forgot to ask if Sindona needed a spacesuit. She debated turning back, but finally decided against it. If the answer was yes, it would only depress Sindona further. Not to mention her and Rex. They'd have to figure out a system of switching suits, just in case.

Quarnian lay in her sleepnet. She was tired, endlessly tired, but she couldn't begin to sleep.

It was all falling apart around her. Bruce had left, Rex was too upset to think straight, and Sindona was going insane. It was all up to her.

She tried hard not to let it bother her. She had done pretty well on her own before. That time on Radis, for instance . . .

The thoughts didn't work. This was different; it seemed centuries since the whole thing began. It was going to take strength to go on, and she wasn't sure she'd be able to find it.

It was ridiculous; they were close to escaping. Just a few more breaks, a few more days, and the three of them would be going back to New Wichatah. She shouldn't be having any trouble finding her enthusiasm.

Instead, she felt sad and alone.

Quietly, she unzipped her sleepnet.

She hesitated outside Rex's door. He was probably asleep; she wasn't sure she wanted to wake him. She decided it would be best to come in gently. As quietly as she could, she opened the door.

Rex wasn't even zipped in. He glared at her.

"I . . . I couldn't sleep," Quarnian said. She felt embarrassed, as if she had been caught stealing a baby's bottle. What had possessed her to come here in the first place? "I wanted to talk with someone."

"Why not Taril?"

"Rex, I told you . . ." She stopped; that line had gotten her nowhere. "Because he's working," she snapped. "Does that satisfy you?"

Rex's eyes drilled into her. "What do you want from me?"

The hostility in his words was like a knife in her gut. She fought against the feeling. "We've got to work together. I can't do that if you hate me."

"Hate you?" Rex laughed without humor. "I wish to God I did."

Quarnian was silent for a moment. "You love me," she mumbled.

Rex looked at her with fierce defiance, and she knew the answer was yes.

"And you're upset about Taril. Look, Rex—"

"I know what you told me. I believed it. You put on a good act back there in the lab."

"Act?" Quarnian stared at him. So now he had convinced himself it was all an act. "Rex, you're . . ." She couldn't bring herself to say the word "crazy."

"It was very good. You syrons are experts at making things seem real. I even believed some of it. But I don't believe any of it anymore."

"Dammit, Rex, it was the truth! What do I have to do to convince you?"

He looked at her, a sneer disfiguring his face. "Anything you want. A syron can make a mere human being believe anything. Can't you?"

Quarnian had nothing to say.

"You wanted to talk," Rex said, breaking the long silence. "Looks like you're done."

Quarnian didn't take the hint. She didn't want to go just yet. "I'm *not* done. I wanted to say . . ." She found she couldn't finish the sentence. What *had* she wanted to say?

"I'm listening."

Quarnian swallowed. "All right, I guess I really didn't want to say anything. I just wanted you to stop being mad at me."

"All right, I'll stop."

"Rex, don't be difficult."

"I mean it. I'll stop; I'll keep my thoughts to myself. I can't promise you anything more."

She sighed. He was right. "I suppose not."

"Fine, then. I'll see you in the morning."

Quarnian made no move to the door; she felt that once she passed through it, too much would have been lost. "Rex, I . . ."

"Get to the point. It's late."

"I'm trying! Do you think this is easy for me?" Quarnian was surprised at her shout. "Rex, you remember the time you thought I needed to be held? I think I need that again."

"Just that?"

She felt her face burning. It was always hard for her to express weakness, and Rex seemed to want even more from her. "Yes, I . . ." She stopped and looked into his face. It was marginally less hostile, as if he knew something she didn't. "You're right, Rex. There *was* something else. Only believe me—I didn't realize it until right this moment."

His expression was noncommittal. "What is it?"

Her cheeks reddened further as she said the words, "I'd like to make love with you."

Rex was silent for a few moments. "Oh?" he asked guardedly. "Do you really mean that?"

"Yes, Rex, I do. I don't love you; I told you that. I'm sorry, I really am. Under different circumstance . . ." She stopped herself; she would have to be completely honest. "No, I shouldn't even hint at that. I *do* want to make love with you, though. It would be a tremendous comfort."

"I don't know. . . . "

"Oh, come on now, Rex. You don't have to love someone to have sex with her. You should know after that swath you cut back on New Wichatah."

"That was different."

"You know it wasn't." Quarnian sighed. "Look, Rex, I'm not going to beg and I'm not going to force you,. I've said all that I can. I hope you believe me when I tell you it wasn't easy. It's up to you now: do you want me to stay or not? Because if you don't, I'm leaving. And I'm not going to ask you about it again." She felt a catch in her voice. "I don't think I'd be able."

The silence seemed to last forever. She kept her eyes on his face. It was a mask, giving nothing away, even to her. Whatever decision he was making, he was giving her no clue.

She realized she was holding her breath.

"Quarn," he said finally, opening his arms wide and invitingly, "come here."

Chapter Twenty

Quarnian felt herself waking up. She hadn't realized that she had drifted off. Stretching slowly, she opened her eyes.

Rex was watching her, his right arm cradling her against the chill of the cabin.

"How long have I been asleep?" she asked.

He shrugged. "I don't know. I've been sleeping myself."

"Probably morning," she mumbled. Reluctantly, she began to pull herself away from him. "I'll have to get to work, I guess. They'll be looking for me."

"Quarn," Rex said tentatively, "maybe you're right. Maybe I *do*—"

She stopped him with a finger on his lips. "Don't say it, Rex. Please don't. It'll drive us both crazy. This is a one-night stand. You're used to them."

"Not like—"

"No, Rex. I meant what I said last night."

He let out a sigh and nodded. "Could this at least have the status of a precedent?"

It took Quarnian a second to get the reference; she laughed. "I'm not promising anything. We may not get a chance again, anyway. But if my feelings are wrong and we

164

don't get out of here . . . well, I'd much rather make a baby with you than with any of the crew here. At least you're human."

"Thanks for the vote of confidence," Rex said, smiling.

She pushed away from him. "You'll just have to add me to your list of conquests." She began putting on her jumpsuit.

Quarnian slowly worked her way toward the spacesuits. She had been lucky; her task was leading her in the right direction. It was a good thing the hydroponics had so much rust.

She neared the door she knew she'd have to go through. Sindona had indicated there was a back exit. Quarnian was glad, since she'd never be able to smuggle anything out under the noses of those working in the garden. She'd just have to pick her moment, hide the suit somewhere, and get back to work before anyone noticed she was gone.

And, of course, the most important thing: she had to pray her luck held out.

She moved along the wall, heading closer to her goal, spreading the silvery fluid and trying to plan. She had already covered most of this side; the area she had done the day before now gleamed in rustless splendor. They should paint it, she told herself before she realized that they probably didn't have any paint.

She reached the storeroom door and began wiping the rust from its frame. It didn't look securely locked and it shouldn't present any problem at all. She slowly reached for the handle.

Without warning, a mass plowed into her back, pounding her against the wall. Her chin cracked onto the metal and she grunted in surprise and pain.

Two legs were straddling her, two hands curled around her throat.

Quarnian pushed and twisted, her fists pounding into her attacker's forearms. It did little good. The grip wasn't overly strong, but the pressure was cutting off her breath. Very soon, it would be deadly.

She managed to spin around. The mass on her back hit

the wall with a satisfying thud, and the grip became a little less tight.

Finding the wall with her feet, Quarnian pushed off with all her strength, twisting violently into a spin.

The hands slipped from her neck.

Quarnian wriggled free from the encompassing legs. Thank the stars for Newton's laws, she thought as she spun around to see her attacker.

It was Rixalt. Her face was almost alien in its anger.

Rixalt? What—?

Quarnian's mind reeled under an onslaught of mental violence. Rixalt had edged to the wall, her feet reaching for it, ready to spring. Quarnian wasn't sure what to do. She tried to sense if the other woman had a weak spot, but could find nothing. She would have to fight, and knew that Rixalt had the advantage in weightlessness.

Quarnian suppressed a shudder. She was so used to having an edge that being at a disadvantage seemed terrifying.

Rixalt was ready to spring. Maybe she could dodge. . . .

And, from nowhere, they were surrounded by crew members, their hands grabbing Rixalt, holding her away, pulling Quarnian away from her.

Let me go! The power of Rixalt's mental scream gave Quarnian a headache.

The captain doesn't want her damaged.

I don't care.

You will. The overtones in the thought were dire. *Leave her alone.*

Rixalt looked at one of the crew members, her eyes locked on his in a test of wills. Then she glanced for a moment at Quarnian and mindspoke. *All right. You can let go of me now.*

The three people holding her slowly let go, their postures tense, as though waiting for her to launch herself at Quarnian again.

Wait, Quarnian thought. *Why did you do it, Rixalt?*

The other woman looked at her with icy eyes, then pushed off away from Quarnian, her trajectory taking her toward the door of the hydroponics.

The sense of relief almost cut through Quarnian's puzzlement.

Better stay away from her, someone thought at her.

Great advice, Quarnian thought. She realized that everyone there was looking at her. *I'm all right, but does anyone know why she did that?*

There were no thoughts projected at her. Quarnian wasn't sure if that meant no one knew or that they didn't dare tell her.

She also realized something else. She shouldn't try to steal the suit that day, not after all that commotion. The people were moving away from her, going back to whatever tasks had occupied them, but she noticed they were watching her and pointing her out to latecomers. She was now the topic of conversation, and if that topic vanished into the storeroom, someone would notice.

She sighed and collected the bottle of silver liquid, then moved to a slash of dull red just past the storeroom door. The movement away from her goal nearly made her wince, but she had no choice. Maybe her chance would come later. Maybe.

A small figure glided toward her as she moved onward. "Lady, are you all right?"

The sound of the voice seemed strange in the stillness of the ship. "Oh, hello, Bruce. Just a little sore. I . . ." And she realized this could be her chance. Bruce had more freedom than she did and, after all, they had gotten into this together. Maybe there was some way to convince him to give her a hand. "It's strange hearing your voice," she said cautiously. "I guess you're having a hard time finding people to talk with."

Bruce shook his head. "They like talking now. A fad."

One line of attack shot down. "I guess you like it here, then."

The smile on his face was enough of an answer. She should have known. After all, she had come here to bring him here. Her instincts couldn't tell her what to say. "Bruce, I . . ."

He looked puzzled. "What, lady?"

"I need your help." The instant the words entered the air,

she felt panic. She couldn't trust Bruce any more than she could trust Vorst; he was a member of the crew now. The very best she could expect was for him to remain neutral. She tried to read him; nothing occurred to her.

Bruce's smile had become a frown. "Lady, I told you . . ."

"Yes, Bruce, you're right. I don't want to involve you with us. I'm . . ." And suddenly, she had a flash. The overtones in his words reverberated in her head. He *was* willing to do something to help; she'd just have to find the right way to ask. "It's just that—"

"Don't talk about it," Bruce snapped. "You won't get my help."

If he *is* willing, Quarnian thought, he isn't aware of it yet. "Bruce, I know you want to join the crew. But how did you get the chance? Who brought you up here?"

"You, lady," Bruce mumbled. His sullenness had returned to earlier levels.

"Don't you think you owe me something for that?"

Bruce was silent; his eyes couldn't meet hers. "What do you want?" he asked abruptly.

She told him about the spacesuit. "Just take it to the airlock by the *Wreckless*; you can stow it in the locker there. That's all; I promise never to ask anything of you again."

"I'll think about it."

"No. We don't have much time left. You'll have to do it today."

"I can't."

"You owe me, Bruce," Quarnian said desperately. "Remember that. I could have left you on New Wichatah. With your friend Smith. Would you have liked that?" She waited a moment to let the question sink in before going on. "This isn't much for me to ask in return. I promise you that no one here will find out you helped us." She fell silent, all her ammunition gone. She had a hunch it might have worked.

Then, for a fearful moment, she thought it was only a false hope. They would never get off. . . .

"All right," Bruce said.

The relief washed over her like a hot shower. "Thank you." She suddenly realized that this might possibly be their last conversation. "And I want to say you're a true friend. And a gentleman."

The smile had returned to the little man's face. "Thanks, lady," he murmured and sped off before the scene could become sloppy.

Too many people in the recycler, thought Sindona, *end up with nothing.*

Sindona, it's Quarnian. Do you understand me? Quarnian was worried; she hadn't been able to get a sensible response in the past five minutes. She had thought Sindona would like a visit; now she was beginning to think it might be too late to save the crew woman's sanity.

*Quarnian, Quarnian, Quarnian . . . *

Sindona, listen to me. It's all right. I'm going to help you.

Sindona made no acknowledgment. Her disconnected babble was disconcerting; Quarnian wondered if it had been a mistake to swear by the star. She wished she could break her promise, but her training erased that idea from her mind. It went against all her instincts; she was going to have to keep working at it.

"Sindona, please," she said, lapsing into speech in the hope it would help. "I have to know if you're all right."

Oh. You are real. Unless you're a hallucination. But I'm fine. Real fine. Terrific. Never felt better.

"Sindona, I need to know . . . can you breathe space?"

Can I? Can I? Of course I can. I've done it a million times. A hundred million times. A million billion times.

"For how long?"

I can do it forever. Forever and ever and ever. Until I die. Sindona projected a sudden mental giggle. *That's funny.*

"Sindona, please. Get a hold of yourself."

I can't hold anything. I can't hold anything. I can't hold anything. The repeated thought brimmed with depression.

Quarnian tried to project calming thoughts. *It'll be all right.*

No. You don't know. I'm going crazy.

You are not going crazy. Quarnian felt a desperate

need to reassure her; it was partly her fault that Sindona was there.

"I'm afraid she is."

Quarnian whirled at the sound of the voice behind her. Taril was grinning at her.

"Scared?" he asked, giving her no hint as to how much he had overheard.

Quarnian decided it hadn't been too much. "You startled me." She remembered what Bruce had said about the crew talking. "I see you've taken up the fad."

"Fad. Fff-a-a-a-d. I like the feel of that word in my mouth. There's a lot to be said for speaking."

"Mmnnn. Look, could you please let Sindona out of there? I'm worried that she—"

"She'll be all right. She's only going crazy now; that's not unusual. About half those in epilepsia can't deal with it; usually high-strung types like Sindona. But we can cure it. There's nothing to worry about."

"But she's suffering. . . . "

"She won't remember any of it. Trust me. I wouldn't do anything to cause permanent damage."

"Because that would be a waste," Quarnian said bitterly.

"Exactly."

There was a smugness in the way he said the word. "I've got to be going," Quarnian mumbled.

Taril blocked her way. "Now, don't be mad. We were getting along so well up to now."

Quarnian felt herself beginning to blush; she hoped it wouldn't show in the dim light.

"You're an attractive woman. Much more interesting than any of the others here. What is a syron?"

"A . . . Where did you hear that word?"

"Sindona keeps babbling about it. Says you're one. What is it?"

"Nothing important. It's a . . . a special type of training. It . . . helps you deal with new situations."

"Like this one?"

She nodded. "Like this one. Now, if you'll please get out of my way. . . . "

"Quarnian, are you upset with me?"

The question puzzled her. "No, of course not." Don't let him suspect her real feelings about him. "I'm just tired."

He looked at her closely; she prayed he couldn't read anything in her expression. "Well, I don't want to upset you. You're a fascinating woman; I feel lucky that our genes are so compatible. I'd like to make you my permanent mate—if that's all right with you," he added hurriedly.

There was an almost shy quality to his voice; she had never heard it before. "You . . . they'd allow you to do that?"

He nodded. "Sometimes. If both parties agree, of course. It is not necessarily for reproduction, but for companionship."

"And you have no companion?"

A touch of red tinged his cheeks. "We can change our minds. There is nothing wrong with that. But I would never change my mind about you." Taril looked at her like a little puppy. "You will agree, won't you?"

Quarnian felt dizzy. "I . . . it's kind of a shock. I'm not thinking straight. Give me some time."

"Certainly. Only . . ."

"Only, what?"

"Only don't be upset about how I treated you at first. I just didn't know anything about human mating customs and I thought—"

"It's all right," Quarnian mumbled. She tried to suppress a smile; there was something very amusing about seeing this space monster with a crush on her. She felt flattered.

Taril moved out of the way. "All right, then. I'm glad we got that straight. I've got to be going."

"Where?"

He smiled at the question. "Not yet. When we become mated, I'll be glad to tell you everything." He disappeared down the corridor.

Quarnian lingered for several moments, wondering why the frast she was so attractive to men. She decided it must be some sort of curse.

"You mean we're going to have to depend on that little—?"

"Rex, be quiet. It was the best I could do. Bruce is dependable."

Rex snorted. "I'd like to be able to check on him."

She shook her head. "We can't. We're just going to have to trust him."

Rex pursed his lips. "All right, what about Sindona? Does she need a suit?"

"She says she doesn't. That's not going to be a problem." She hoped the words sounded confident enough to fool him. She made no mention of Sindona's mental state.

"All right, then. Let's get started; the sooner we're away, the better." He reached into a storage locker and pulled out the epilyzer.

She grabbed his hand. "Rex, we've already discussed that."

He held up the weapon. "I'd still like to give them a taste of their own medicine."

"Do you know how to work it?"

Rex looked disgusted. "It's a weapon. I'll figure it out."

"But it works two ways: it disables you and it cures you. How can you be sure it's set the right way?"

"A test then. Hold still."

"No!" The weapon aimed at her gave her a terrible fear; the memory of what it had done before was too strong. "I mean, it would still be useless to us. We've got to be sure we knock them unconscious."

"Or kill them."

Rex's words gave Quarnian a chill. "Or kill them," she repeated. "But I'd like to avoid that, if possible."

"Why? We're fighting for survival. I'm sure you've killed people before."

The last sentence hurt the most. "You think it's easy to kill someone?"

"But syrons are supposed to—"

"I'm not talking about physical ability. Those are still other human beings out there. Maybe you can forget that, but I can't."

"But we may need to . . ."

"I've killed men, Rex. Three of them. Each one was about to kill me when I got him. Pure self-defense. But I still remember their faces, the way they looked at the very last instants of their lives. They realized they were dying. They were tough men, but the fear that covered their faces . . . it was the most frightening thing I've ever seen." The faces returned to her memory as she talked. She had tried to forget them for so long that she had almost succeeded. Almost. "You're used to cowboys and Indians. Bang and everyone falls down. Let me tell you, Rex, killing is about as much fun as dying."

There was a long silence. Rex slowly floated in the room, staring at her. "What . . . what do you want me to do?" he asked, his voice subdued.

"I don't know. I'll have to disable the guards somehow. I'll think of something."

"You'd better."

She took the epilyzer from him. "We're still going to have to figure out how to work this. For Sindona." She studied the weapon. There was a button protruding from its handle, and it seemed to slide along a track. Trigger and reverse control all in one. Only which was which?

She would have to make a guess. Most likely forward for stun, backward for reverse. She hoped she was right; no telling what a double dose of epilepsia would do. She doubted it would be beneficial.

"All right," she said, pocketing the weapon. "I think I've got it."

Rex nodded.

"Now, we're going to have to move fast. As soon as the guard comes to, we're done for. He'll raise an alarm and they'll be at the airlock in half a minute. We can't afford to waste even a second."

"I wasn't planning on taking a tour of the ship."

The line brought a smile to Quarnian's lips. "Go straight to the airlock with the airstone. I'll get Sindona. Get out and fill the *Wreckless*; I'm not sure how long she'll be able to go without air."

"Didn't she tell you?"

"No. We were . . . interrupted. I'll get my suit and meet you on the *Wreckless*. And if it doesn't look like I'm going to make it—"

"You will."

"If I don't," Quarnian went on, "leave without me. You can send help from New Wichatah."

"Quarn . . ."

"Do it, Rex. I'll manage until you get back."

"And when you make it to the *Wreckless*?"

Quarnian grinned. " 'When'? Not 'if'? Well, I think you can guess what to do."

"Get away from here," Rex mumbled.

"As quickly as possible. We'll worry about adjusting our course later."

"If we can. You know what our fuel situation was."

Quarnian sighed. "If we worried about every little thing, we might as well set up camp on the *Staroamer*. Let's go; we don't have forever."

"Quarn?" Rex asked. "You *are* sure we're going to get back to New Wichatah?"

"Of course, I'm . . ." She looked at him, then shook her head. "No, I'm not sure. I don't know if my feelings are correct or not. I guess I never had any real hunches about it at all—just pessimism or wishful thinking."

"Then why did you—?"

"It sure beats doing nothing, doesn't it?" Quarnian said. "Come on, we've got a lot to accomplish."

Chapter Twenty-one

They made their way as silently as possible, hoping no one would see them. At best, being discovered now would force them to delay things until some better time. At worst, it would alert Vorst to increase security.

Quarnian patted the epilyzer as she glided along, trying to form a plan. She was used to making things up as she went along, but this time she wasn't confident enough to just barge in and trust her luck. As soon as they turned up the corridor to the storage area, the guards would see them. There was no place to hide, only ten meters or so of straight corridor. Even if the guards were looking the other way, there was no guarantee she'd be able to get to them in time.

And she needed time. Time to get near, time to discover their spot of weakness. That could take too long; you can only find it by observation. Some people don't even have one.

She thought about trying a brick to the back of the head—not fancy, but still effective. But out of the question; they would have to deliver two blows simultaneously. Quarnian doubted that they'd be able to get enough force behind them anyway; it's hard moving objects when you have nothing to brace against.

Frast, there was even the possibility that the airstones weren't even in there. . . .

Quarnian shook her head. If you worried about everything . . . Her mind went back to her Training. "Trust your instincts," they had said. "They'll get you out of most anything."

She took the words to heart, trying to ignore the "most."

They reached the branch to the storeroom without being detected. Quarnian paused and signaled to Rex to stop.

Quarnian cleared her mind to see what they were up against.

She could only pick up far-off snatches of conversation. She frowned; it was all much too faint to be the guards. She waited, hoping she had come in during a lull. What else did they have to do but talk?

"What's the matter?" Rex whispered. His lips were millimeters from her ear; the warmth of his breath was disconcerting.

She told him, speaking as softly as she could.

"Maybe they took the guards away."

Quarnian nodded, but she didn't believe it.

There was only one way to find an answer; she indicated that Rex should stay where he was.

There was a guard, a solitary man. Evidently they had decided not to spare any others. It would make things a trifle easier.

Her movement must have attracted his eye; before she could pull herself back to make plans, he saw her.

And she recognized him: Taril.

"Quarnian!"

She decided the best thing to do was to act innocent. She moved forward. "Hello. I was looking for you."

Taril looked suspicious. "Why?"

"I . . ." She tried to read him to get a handle on his thoughts; nothing came. She'd have to play it by ear. "I . . ."

Taril raised his epilyzer and regarded her warily. "Yes?"

"I hope I'm not bothering you. . . ."

"No." He smiled. "As a matter of fact, you're making my job worthwhile."

She caught several meanings in his words; she wasn't sure

which one he had intended. "I'm sorry if I'm not making much sense. This is hard for me to say." That sounded good.

"What is?" His grip on the weapon had not relaxed.

"Well ... I've been thinking about what you said to me before. About ... permanently mating."

"And?" He seemed to be lowering his guard.

She took a deep breath and swam slightly nearer; he didn't seem to notice. "Well ... I think it might be nice."

Taril didn't say a thing; a smile crossed his face. It was different from his earlier grins, softer, perhaps happier. He projected his thoughts at her.

"My God," Quarnian whispered. They almost embarrassed her. She could feel his affection warming her like a cozy fire. It enveloped her in well-being; she understood every bit of his feelings toward her.

"Quarnian?"

She shook her head; it had seemed that she was a part of his emotion for a very long time. "I'm sorry. I was overwhelmed. I'm used to spoken language; it seems so clumsy now."

He projected more sweet thoughts at her. She smiled; this could become addicting. The best she could project was an *I love you, too.*

It was a mistake. Taril frowned. "That doesn't sound like you mean it."

"I'm sorry. I ... I'm still not very good at it." An idea came to her. "Here, let me show you." She advanced.

"What ... ?"

He was aiming his epilyzer at her, but she had her arms around him. As the weapon lowered, she began to kiss him with all the emotion she could pretend.

Slowly, she felt his suspicion weaken.

Now was the time. She pressed his neck gently, her fingers moving in the precise rhythm.

He pushed away, smiling. "You're some woman. I must—"

And then, suddenly, it hit.

She could feel the questions in his mind as he began to lose consciousness. His eyelids drooped. Quarnian prayed he didn't have the strength left to call for help.

He managed to keep his eyes open. His face looked lost and betrayed; his pain tore at her. "You . . ." he managed to whisper.

I'm sorry, Taril. I truly am, she projected at him.

He gave no indication he had received the thought. He felt limp in her arms.

She pushed him aside. "Rex!" she whispered as loudly as she could as she went to work on the storeroom's lock.

He got there just as she was opening it. "Is he . . . ?"

"He'll be out about an hour," Quarnian said, trying to put Taril's expression out of her mind. She checked her watch, noting the time. "Give or take a few minutes. Let's hurry. Once he comes to, it's all over for us."

The storeroom was dark, lit only by the dull glow that spilled over from the corridor. They pushed Taril inside to hide him.

Quarnian glanced around. "Let's find that air. Look for a ball of some sort."

The room was large and they could only see shadows. The seconds sped by, turning with frightening rapidity into minutes. Quarnian rushed from place to place, trying to be thorough, yet afraid she had missed what she wanted, but too rushed to go back to double-check. And the thought crept into her mind that they had only guessed that the airstones were in here. . . .

After ten excruciating minutes, Rex called from the far side of the compartment. "Are these them?"

He pointed to four roundish lumps floating deep within the room.

Quarnian propelled herself over and rubbed a hand over them. The texture seemed soft and convoluted, as though millions of channels and pathways had been carved into the plastic. "This is it," she said.

"How many do we need?"

"One should be enough—assuming it's full."

"How can we tell?"

"I don't know. Maybe there's a change of color or something." She pushed one toward the light to see better; it was a dirty gray. She nodded and pulled at another.

It didn't budge.

She jerked at it again. It was as though it were tied down. Then, slowly it began to move. "This is it," she said. "It's a lot more massive than the other; that has to be because it's full. Help me."

As the two of them wrestled the mass around, Quarnian glanced around the room. She spotted a metal container the size of a vacuum bottle clipped to the wall. It was labeled with the letter C. She grabbed it, hoping abbreviations hadn't changed in five hundred years.

They wrestled the stone out the door. "Think you can handle that alone?" she asked.

"Sure."

"Fine. Take it to the airlock." She handed him the container after unscrewing its top to make sure she had guessed right. "Here's the carbon for the catalyst. Fill up the *Wreckless*. We'll be with you soon." She handed him the epilyzer she had been carrying. "Use this if you're seen. It'll buy you some time. And if it looks like they know you're in the *Wreckless*, don't bother waiting for me. Get out."

"Quarn, I can't—"

"Do as I say." On sudden impulse, she leaned over and kissed him. "That's in case I don't make it. Now get going."

Rex opened his mouth, thought better of it, and began to push the mass of the airstone.

Quarnian checked the time. A quarter of it was now gone. She swam over to Taril, taking his epilyzer, then began to push away, but some instinct stopped her. She frowned, then patted Taril's pockets. After a moment, she discovered what she was looking for: a ring of keys. It would come in handy. Pocketing them, she headed for Sindona's cell.

It seemed to take forever to reach the cell area. She tried not to rush, but found it impossible to move slowly. Luckily, she ran into only two crew members along the way. They merely smiled as she passed. It was a good sign: no alarm yet.

She was almost to the cells when she felt a sudden certainty that something was wrong ahead of her. She slowed, then cautiously peered into the corridor that ran outside the cells.

Someone was there.

Her reflexes took over. Quarnian pressed herself into a shadow. A flange of metal about ten centimeters wide, the edge of a doorway, was all that she had for cover.

Cautiously, she glanced at who was ahead.

It was Vorst. He was floating in front of Sindona's cell, peering in thoughtfully, studying Sindona carefully. He leaned forward, then pulled back and appeared to think, taking his time with every movement.

Quarnian checked the time, feeling irritated. Less than forty minutes left now. And they'd need time to get to the airlock. . . .

Vorst continued to think. His motions were deliberate, as though he was trying to make a decision.

What was he *doing* there? Quarnian thought. What—? She stopped herself just in time; she had nearly projected the thought.

Then Vorst nodded.

Quarnian felt a flash of relief, but it was quickly damped. Vorst had taken a key and opened the cell door. He disappeared inside.

She wondered what to do next, but knew her only option was to wait.

Quarnian stared at the open door; it hid her view of inside, and she didn't dare leave her hiding place for a closer look. She kept searching for a sign of movement, an indication that Vorst was leaving, but saw only the mute metal door.

The minutes passed.

She felt helpless. She didn't think she'd be able to jump Vorst, and she was sure she couldn't disable him. She could only try to be patient, to forget that Taril would soon be awake.

Then, finally, she saw some movement. Vorst emerged from the cell, and Quarnian was able to breathe again. The captain seemed relieved. Quarnian realized the reason for his concern: Sindona was a member of the crew. He couldn't stand to see her harmed, even if he had ordered the epilepsia for everyone's good. It figured he'd be softhearted. Life was precious out here.

Vorst locked the door and put away the key. He made a move to go.

Then he stopped. He looked again in Sindona's cell.

Come on, thought Quarnian. *Come on.*

Vorst's head jerked back and Quarnian pressed herself farther into the shadows. She dared not look, dared not breathe, dared not even think. . . .

She heard nothing.

She didn't know how long she remained frozen. All she knew was that time was passing. She would have to look.

Vorst was gone.

Evidently he hadn't known the mindspeaker was her. And she knew that you can't zero in on a thought the way you can with sound. He probably supposed it came from another direction.

Quarnian spent no more time thinking. She leaped forward to reach Sindona, the ring of Taril's keys already in her hand. There were eight of them. She fumbled through them, searching for the one that fit. The sixth key opened the door.

Sindona was asleep. Quarnian gently nudged her. It set off a shock wave of convulsions. She had forgotten the effect of the epilyzer. *Sindona, are you all right?*

The return thought was confused and logy, as though emerging from a drugged calm. *Thing of dreams. They are after my archives. Must bite . . . *

No help at all. Quarnian lifted Taril's epilyzer, moving the slide to what she thought was the right position, and pressed the button.

Sindona's quivering stopped.

Quarnian felt her heart stop along with it. Had she killed her? *Sindona?*

There was no answer for a terrifying instant, then a befuddled thought. *Archives more power.*

Quarnian was able to breathe again. *You're all right now, Sindona. You can move.*

I can move. The thought was dull.

Yes. Come with me. I'm going to get you out of here.

Quarnian? Quarnian, is that you?

Yes. Don't try to mindspeak.

I can move, Quarnian. What a wonderful dream.

It's not a dream. Now be quiet. We've got to get out of here.

Sindona darted out the cell, dancing in midair. *I can move, I can move, I can—*

Quiet! For an instant, Quarnian thought about leaving her there. She shook her head at the idea. *Let's go, Sindona. But be sure to do what I say.*

Whatever you say.

There was a fragile quality in the way Sindona thought and moved, a strained dottiness as though the least little stress would shatter her. Quarnian doubted she'd be any help if there was any trouble. It was possible she'd never be completely sane without the measures available aboard the *Staroamer*.

But, sane or not, Sindona was going to New Wichatah.

Quarnian led her into the corridors, the dark, untraveled ones where they would stand less chance of being discovered. She did not look at her watch, knowing the truth would only depress her.

She tried to hurry, but Sindona slowed her like an anchor dragging behind her. She would stare at shadows, or mutter a few inaudible words and then giggle. Quarnian began to feel as if she were in a dream, one of those where you run and run and run and never get anywhere. She wondered what sort of alarm system Taril might use and felt uncomfortably sure she would be hearing it any second.

Then she heard the mindspeech.

Quarnian froze. From the strength of the thought, it was nearby. No one should be in the abandoned corridor, not so late in the shift. But someone was and Quarnian could sense whoever it was coming her way.

She glanced around quickly. A door stood to her right. The handle turned and it opened with a tiny creak that seemed to echo through the corridor like a shout. She pulled Sindona in with her and gently shut the door. There wasn't much room. The space was little more than a closet.

Quarnian listened.

Her ears found nothing, but she could sense a voice in her mind. *She has no right,* it said. *I should have killed her.*

The tones were familiar, with the same violence she had sensed in the hydroponics. Rixalt.

Quarnian could tell the woman was coming nearer. Her inexplicable fury was like a marker, getting stronger as she approached.

"Quarnian?" Sindona asked.

Quarnian suppressed an urge to curse. "Quiet," she whispered, her mouth close to her companion's ear. "Don't say anything."

All right. I'm not speaking now.

"Don't even mindspeak," Quarnian hissed, but it was already too late. She could sense a questioning thought outside the door. She reached for the epilyzer.

The door opened and Rixalt regarded her.

Quarnian had the epilyzer aimed. All she had to do was push the button, but the image of Sindona twitching helplessly came vividly to mind. And the memory of her own helplessness. . . .

You're escaping, Rixalt thought. There was no disapproval in the statement.

Quarnian didn't answer. Her feelings told her to wait.

Go, thought Rixalt. *Get away from here.* There was a slight pause. *And leave my Taril alone.*

And suddenly everything fit. Taril had spoken of a companion.

"Go!" Rixalt said, lapsing into speech.

Quarnian didn't wait for another invitation. "Come on, Sindona."

They started away, but she could not avoid looking back. "It wasn't my idea," she said to Rixalt. "I didn't want to come between—"

"Leave!"

Quarnian didn't say anything more. Matters would have to go unexplained. She urged Sindona onward to the airlock.

They reached the airlock without any more close calls. Rex was waiting for them, suited up, the airstone already in the lock.

"I told you to—" Quarnian began.

"Damned little runt didn't bring the suit. There was only one here."

Quarnian felt a sinking feeling. "Are you sure?"

"Of course I'm sure. I told you we couldn't trust—"

"All right, all right. Let me think." Nothing came. All she could think of was Bruce. Why had he changed his mind?

Rex pointed at Sindona. "What's the matter with her?"

So it was that obvious. "Nothing. She's just a little disoriented. We're going to have to—"

A wailing like a voice in pain interrupted her. Quarnian stiffened. She now knew what the alarm sounded like.

"What the frast?" Rex asked.

"Rex, get to the airlock. They'll be here in a minute."

"I'm not leaving without you."

The wailing seemed to get louder. "Rex, don't be an idiot. You can send help when you reach New Wichatah. Go!"

"Not without you."

"Rex, you stubborn—"

"Lady?"

It was Bruce. He was at the head of the airlock area, holding Quarnian's spacesuit. "They moved it," he grunted. "Had to search. Here." He left the suit floating in midair and pushed off down the corridor.

Quarnian was the first to move. "Get Sindona in the airlock," she said, going for the suit. "I'll change inside."

She grabbed the suit and rebounded off the nearest wall, her trajectory now straight for the airlock door. Rex had Sindona inside already. Quarnian joined them and, almost as though the movement had been rehearsed, Rex shut the door behind her.

"Get into that suit," he said. He was grinning.

Quickly but cautiously, Quarnian put it on, double-checking to make sure everything was airtight. It wouldn't do to forget a seal just because she was in a hurry.

There was still no sign of any of the crew. They seemed to be taking their time getting there. Quarnian didn't wonder why; she knew better than to question good luck.

Finally, she was ready. "Can you hear me?" she asked into her radio.

"Fine. Let's go."

How about you, Sindona?

There was a giggle in her mind. *This is fun. Where are we going?*

Quarnian could see another advantage of mindspeech on the *Staroamer:* less clumsy than radios. *Outside.* She grabbed her arm. "OK, Rex."

Rex pressed the evacuation switch.

Quarnian felt a sense of relief. "Good," she said. "With any luck, we'll be out of here before they get to us."

"I don't think so," Rex said, his eyes on the pressure gauge. "The air's not draining."

Chapter Twenty-two

Quarnian stared at the pressure gauge, trying to wish it lower. The needle didn't budge at all. "They'll be here in a few minutes," she said to Rex. "Is there anything we can do?"

Rex looked at the door leading back to the ship. "I can probably jam that. It'll hold them off for a little while."

Quarnian nodded. "Do it. We need the time to think." She began to look around the airlock as though there might be clues written on the walls. There was nothing distinguishing about it; airlocks were airlocks, even if they were five hundred years old. Just a closet with two doors, with intakes to create a vacuum.

She looked at Sindona. *Can you turn off the alarm?*

The walls in here are pretty, don't you think? Green is such a restful color. Are there really meters and meters of it on Earth?

Quarnian didn't answer; she doubted that Sindona would notice. Her eyes hit upon the exit door. Just one piece of metal between them and freedom. If only the lock was working. . . .

And then she realized what she was overlooking. She

swore; she had begun to think like a member of the crew. It didn't matter if they wasted the air in there or not. "Rex, could you break down that door?"

Rex looked at her and then at the door. "Maybe—if I had some tools. But it's built to be strong. I doubt we can do it." He pulled at the manual wheel; it didn't move. "Standard," he mumbled. "It won't open if there's air in here."

"So we've got to find a way to get rid of the air. . . . Rex, the airstone!"

"What about it?"

"We can use that. If we heat it, it'll absorb the air in here. Then we can open the door. Find something to—"

A good plan, Quarnian, but it won't work. The stone is already saturated.

Who . . . Vorst!

Yes. I must admit I underestimated you. You had us pretty well fooled. But then, we knew you'd have to come through here if you wanted to get out.

Quarnian didn't reply. She should have sensed it: the freedom they had been given, the time it took for Vorst to reach the other side of the lock. The crew didn't have to worry. Whatever she and Rex tried, they'd have to come through this airlock. Vorst just made sure that the bottleneck was plugged and went about his business.

"Quarnian? What's the matter?"

She looked at Rex. "It's Vorst. He's probably just inside the ship."

You are a very resourceful woman, Quarnian.

Resourceful enough so that you'll let us go?

You know better than that. We need resourceful people on ship, too. Now, open the lock.

You really think I will?

She felt Vorst's mind give off a mental sigh. *No. But you have no choice. You can't live in there indefinitely. I promise there'll be no punishment for this escape attempt. And we'll even cure Sindona.*

I'm fine, I'm perfect.

Quarnian sent a message for Sindona to keep quiet. *We're only going to go through one of these doors. The one that leads to the *Wreckless.**

There was a short pause. *I thought you might feel that way. All right, let me tell you one more thing. Sindona can't breathe space.*

Of course I can. I can do anything. I can—

She says she can, Quarnian thought.

Who would you rather believe: her or me? She's never been out without a suit; it wasn't necessary.

Then you can't be sure.

There was another pause. *No, we can't,* Vorst thought, a sinister overtone to his words. *We never tested her; there was no need for it. But her breeding seems to indicate she can't go out. I know you two are friends; I'm sure you wouldn't want to have her death on your conscience.*

Quarnian felt all her energy drain out of her.

Oh, Sindona thought, *I don't mind.*

Vorst's thoughts were silent.

"What's going on?" Rex asked.

Quarnian welcomed the interruption; she told him what Vorst had been saying.

Rex swore. "Damn it, Quarn, I told you I didn't want to take her."

"All right," Quarnian snapped. "Forget that. Try breaking down that door; we're getting out of here."

You're going to listen to her? Vorst's thought was colored yellow with amazement. *She's not thinking straight, you know.*

I am, too. Very straight. Straight as a corridor. Straight as an arrow. What's an arrow?

You see?

I don't care, Vorst. If she dies, she dies. I think she'd rather be dead than a part of your crew. But we're going to get out of here.

Vorst took a moment to answer. *I suppose you think you'll find a way to open the door.*

Of course.

Fine, try your tricks. We'll be waiting for you when you decide to stop being foolish.

"It's no use," Rex said, trying the outer door again. "I can't budge it."

Quarnian nodded slowly. "We're safe for the moment; they can't get at us. All we have to do is think of a way out."

"Try the door again," Quarnian said, her voice weary but tense.

"I've been trying for nearly an hour. It's no use. They probably have someone waiting outside for us anyway."

Quarnian shook her head. "No. That would waste manpower. They're positive we're not going to be able to get out."

"I'm beginning to believe them, too."

She glared at him and, with a sigh, he went back to work on the door.

Sindona had fallen asleep again. Quarnian didn't bother to wake her; if they did open the door, it might be best if she never found out what had happened. Quarnian hoped she would survive; only a few minutes would be enough. But unpleasant facts had to be faced.

Quarnian stared at the lock again. They hadn't removed their spacesuits, just in case the outer door unexpectedly opened. They had until their air ran out; after that, their chances of escape would reach zero.

Her eyes stopped at one of the few landmarks on the blank green walls: the pressure gauge. It still pointed to normal, mocking her. She wanted to reach out and pull that damned needle down to zero. Then she could . . .

Quarnian started. "Rex," she asked, her pulse racing at the germ of a thought forming, "what has to happen for that door to open?"

He looked at her as though she were as crazy as Sindona. "The pressure in here has got to be . . .." He stopped as he saw where she was staring. "The gauge," he whispered.

"It's electronic, right? There must be some way to short-circuit it; then the door would behave as if the air *was* gone." She had moved over to the gauge as she talked. She pulled at it; the ancient plastic pulled away from the wall.

"Here," Rex said, "let me have it." He took it from her and began to stare at the wiring.

In the background, Quarnian felt the thoughts of the crew. In her excitement, she had forgotten to keep control of her own thoughts. Orders were being given to send out some space breathers. "Hurry, Rex," Quarnian whispered.

"Get to the door," Rex said. "Open it when I tell you."

Quarnian took up her station. She watched as he silently fiddled, praying he'd figure it out soon.

"Damn old equipment," Rex muttered.

Quarnian tried to overhear the thoughts outside. She wished she knew how long it would take to get someone outside; she had no idea how near to the *Wreckless* the spacebreathers would emerge. Silently, she urged Rex on.

"I think I have it," he said finally. "When I press these two wires together, spin the wheel."

Quarnian nodded and looked at Sindona. *Forgive me,* she thought at the sleeping figure. *I did my best.*

"Now!"

Quarnian tugged at the wheel. It spun easily. Soon the door would be—

The air in the lock exploded outward. Quarnian felt her shoulders snap as the door wrenched her forward. The next thing she knew, she had banged into the metal side of the *Wreckless*.

And her mind was filled with thoughts of horror, drowning out the pain of her collision. Sindona was awake and was broadcasting pure, inarticulate terror.

Quarnian tried to project thoughts to calm her, but they were useless against the raw emotions bombarding her. It felt as if a million hammers were banging on the inside of her skull. She closed her eyes against the onslaught.

Rex's voice crackled over the radio. "Get inside!"

The normality of the sound gave her strength. She opened her eyes and looked for Sindona. She was just outside the *Wreckless*'s airlock, flailing away at the vacuum. Her thoughts were becoming more specific: she was urging herself to keep her eyes shut and hold her breath, but her emotions dominated the logic like a sun dominating its planets.

"Let's *go*," Rex said. "We've got to get her inside."

Quarnian nodded. As long as Sindona was thinking, it was a good sign. She pulled herself along the side of the *Wreckless*, toward its airlock and safety.

A hand came out of nowhere, grasping her foot. Quarnian looked down, surprised.

A pale, pasty face looked at her, its teeth grinning in the naked space.

Close up, the spacebreather looked something other than human. His skin was almost transparent. Quarnian could see veins and arteries like markings of ink under its waxy surface. The eyes were large and bulging, magnified by goggles. Tiny flaps of skin closed off the nostrils and he seemed to have no ears.

He began to pull her away from the *Wreckless*.

Quarnian kicked, but could not dislodge the grip. She reached for the epilyzer, trying to overcome her misgivings, knowing she probably couldn't.

The spacebreather started at the sight of the weapon and fear crossed his features. Quarnian realized that to lose control out here would mean death.

The grip on her leg seemed looser. Quarnian kicked—and was free. She managed to pull herself into the *Wreckless*.

"Come *on*," Rex said, the words filled with impatience and fear. "What were you waiting for?"

"Shut the door; we'll talk later." Quarnian tried to pull Sindona into the cabin. It was like fighting a wild animal. Sindona was too panicked to understand anything about what was going on.

Rex slammed shut the door and secured it.

Quarnian tried to calm Sindona. Obviously, she had some ability to contain her breath in a vacuum, but there was no way of knowing for how long.

Rex wrestled the airstone into place and began to reach for the carbon.

And suddenly, Quarnian knew it was wrong, all wrong. "Don't," she shouted at Rex.

"Are you crazy? Take a look at her. She needs—"

"I know." Quarnian felt tears of stress coming to her eyes. "I also know it would be terribly wrong." She wanted to do something, anything, but didn't know what. "Damn these hunches, anyway."

"Quarn, I'm going to—"

"Just a minute. Let me think." Sindona's panic was

weaker in her mind. Quarnian prayed that that didn't mean it was the end. Sindona needed air, and fast. The only source was the airstone. But Quarnian was sure ... "The airstone!"

"Quarn, we can't waste—"

"Just a second. We've got to seal off the cargo area, the cabins—everything but the main control room. The doors *are* airtight, aren't they?"

"Of course they are, but I don't—"

"Do it!"

She was already moving when she said the words. Sindona's thoughts were becoming less and less distinct. If she let the air out of her lungs, it would be over. It was a miracle she had survived these few moments already.

Quarnian got two of the doors, Rex the others. "All right," she said, hoping her stupidity hadn't cost Sindona her life.

For agonizing seconds, nothing happened. A sudden thought struck her: it might take some time for the airstone to work. Too much time. She wished she could know, but it was out of her hands. *It'll be all right,* she thought at Sindona, not knowing whether she believed the words herself.

"Will she make it?" Rex asked.

Quarnian shrugged. "I don't know. We cut it pretty close."

"Then why the delay? She needed air."

Quarnian nodded. "But the airstone only soaks up oxygen. And oxygen is only about a fifth of the atmosphere. If we had tried to fill the whole ship with it, the pressure would have been much too low. It would have done us no good at all."

Rex blinked and didn't say anything.

Quarnian projected soothing thoughts at Sindona. All she got back was a weak, confused garble. Then, suddenly, one clear thought.

I'm breathing!

The wonder in it was almost funny.

"We've got air, Rex," Quarnian said, removing her helmet. The air in the *Wreckless* had a sharp tang to it, a clean contrast to the musty aroma that had dominated the *Staroamer*. "Let's get out of here before they figure out a way to stop us."

Rex was already at the controls; the rockets began to rumble. It was the most beautiful sound Quarnian had ever heard. She felt them accelerate, slowly at first, then picking up more speed until they broke out of the dark bay to see the stars.

She went to look at Sindona. She was unconscious, but otherwise seemed to be all right. Quarnian thought it best to leave her that way; the rest would do her good.

Rex was checking his instruments. "We're in luck; we're heading pretty close to New Wichatah. It won't take much fuel to correct our course."

Quarnian shook her head.

"Is something wrong?"

Quarnian smiled. "No, no. It's just that I'm not sure how to react to good news."

Rex smiled back. "It's been awhile."

"Too long. What I need now . . ."

Vorst suddenly appeared in the cabin, popping out of nothing. He stood before them, slightly translucent.

"How did he . . . ?" Rex began.

Quarnian hushed him; she had learned by now never to underestimate the crew's science.

The voice of the captain came from all around them. "If you don't return immediately," he said, "we will destroy your ship."

Chapter Twenty-three

Rex looked at Quarnian. "Can he do it?"

She shrugged. "I don't even know how he showed up in here." She turned to face Vorst's image; she had no doubt he was able to see her. "Why are you doing this?"

"You'll bring others; they'll find our location and destroy us."

Quarnian sighed. The same old ruts. "I wish you'd get over that. If you want, we won't tell anyone."

"What?" Rex blurted. "And lose—?"

Her glare shut him up; it was the wrong time to mention the reward.

"I'd like to believe you," Vorst said, "but I have the lives of the crew to remember. We're too different; you humans would want to eliminate us."

"I wouldn't even—"

"Not you personally; I know that. But there are others; they might not be as understanding as you. I'm sorry, but I have no choice."

"That's a lot of bull and you know it."

The captain looked puzzled. "I don't see what this has to do with an Earth quadruped."

"Never mind." Quarnian looked at Rex. "Any ideas?" she whispered, hoping that Vorst couldn't hear. "He sounds awfully determined."

Rex shrugged. "All I know is that if he has such a great weapon, why the frast does he worry about being discovered?"

"You're just one unarmed ship," Vorst answered. "We don't have the power to hold off a fully armed fleet indefinitely."

"But, Vorst—"

"Enough talk. You have five minutes. If you haven't changed your course back to the *Staroamer* by then, we will be forced to kill you. I would regret you making me have to do that." He vanished.

"Frast," Quarnian whispered under her breath.

Rex looked at the controls. "I don't think we have the fuel for any evasive action. If we only knew if he really did have a weapon. . . ."

"He does."

They turned to the voice behind them. Sindona was watching, shivering gently.

"Are you all right?" Quarnian asked.

"Fine. It's a bit cold in here, but I'm beginning to warm up."

"How's this mystery weapon work?" Rex asked.

"Depends on which one he's using. They've been as busy inventing weapons as they have been with everything else. It passes the time." Sindona reached for her forehead; her eyelids flickered for a moment. "Sorry. I feel weak. How did I get here, anyway?"

Quarnian looked at her. Evidently the shock of her passage through vacuum had brought her back to her senses. "You don't know?"

"The last thing I remember clearly was being in that cell. Then everything gets sort of fuzzy. . . ." A sudden frown clouded her face. "I seem to remember . . . Did I come through vacuum to get here?"

Quarnian didn't answer.

A twitch of terror ran across Sindona's face. "Quarnian, you could have—"

"We'll discuss this later," Rex jumped in hurriedly.
"After we figure a way out of this."

Quarnian was glad for the interruption. "The best we can
do is try and run for it."

"Is that all?" Rex asked.

"Would you like to go back?"

Rex paused for a moment. "I don't know what other
choice . . ."

"I'm open to suggestions." Quarnian cursed inwardly;
Rex's caution was coming to the fore. "But I don't—"

"Three minutes," crackled Vorst's voice as he popped into
the cabin again, startling the three of them. He disappeared
as soon as the words were uttered.

Rex glared at the empty space; Quarnian couldn't even do
that. Helplessness welled through her. "I guess," she whispered, "there's nothing we can do."

"So we go back?" Rex asked.

Quarnian shook her head; the very idea filled her with
disgust. "We can try to make a run for it. Maybe we'll make
it. If we can't . . ." She shrugged. "We can't. But we're not
going back."

Rex's glower focused on her. "So you want to dare them
to waste us?"

"Rex, I . . ." Quarnian stopped as his words sank in.
"That's it!"

"What do—?"

She shushed him and waited for Vorst to reappear, mar-
shaling her words carefully. It seemed to take forever; each
moment was stretched like a rubber band.

Finally, the captain popped in.

"Vorst!" Quarnian shouted before he could open his
mouth. "You're not going to do anything to us!"

There was a short pause. "I'm sure Sindona told you I can
destroy you."

"But you're not going to. It will be wasting what's most
precious to you: people's lives. And I know how much you
hate to waste anything."

Vorst seemed thoughtful.

Quarnian remembered him hovering outside Sindona's
cell, his face twisted in concern. "Captain, we're three

human beings. You're not the type to kill anyone, for any reason. You've spent your life preserving life."

"I will be saving many more than I . . . waste," Vorst replied tersely, with an overtone of disgust as he pronounced the last word. "It is regrettable, but I will just have to live with it."

"I don't think you'll be able to. Think about me, and Rex, and Sindona. We're people and you're just throwing us away. Besides, you don't really think we'd put the *Staroamer* in jeopardy? None of us wants to be responsible for your deaths, either."

"One minute," Vorst said, putting an end to the discussion.

Rex reached for the controls.

Quarnian grabbed his hands before he could touch anything. "What are you doing?"

He tried to pull away, but her grip was just strong enough to hold him. "Damn it, Quarn, he's got us. Maybe we can get away some other time."

"You know we won't get another chance."

"I'd rather be alive on the *Staroamer* than dead out here. I'm funny that way."

"He's not going to blast us."

Rex looked at her. "Damn it, Quarn, I've been going along with your premonitions, but I'm not going to get myself killed because of them."

The words hurt; he was right. Dying for freedom sounded so noble until you were forced to do it. She let go of his hands. "You're right, Rex," she mumbled.

"It's too late," Sindona said very quietly. "Our time is up."

They froze. Quarnian found herself staring at Rex, trying to say something, anything to be sure he wasn't upset at her for getting him into this. She hated having to die without knowing.

Vorst suddenly appeared again. "All right, Quarnian. You win."

The tons of guilt on her shoulders were suddenly gone. "Thank you, Captain," she mumbled.

"But I want one thing in return."

Sindona grabbed Quarnian's arm. "He wants me. Don't let him . . ."

"What is it?" Quarnian asked.

"Keep the *Staroamer* a secret; tell everyone you traveled in some other direction. Promise me that; I know I can trust your word."

Quarnian nodded as she felt Sindona's hands loosening. "All right, I . . ." A sudden thought occurred to her. "No, I don't promise anything."

"What?" Rex and Sindona screamed together.

"You're still within range," Vorst reminded her.

"I don't promise anything—yet. First, listen to me. Aren't you tired of endlessly conserving every molecule you have? Wouldn't you like to go on your journey without having to worry about every bit of energy?"

"Of course, but—"

"You have a lot to offer the human race. Your science . . ."

"They'll attack us; they'd fear us."

"Perhaps. I don't disagree with you; people are just as fearful and bigoted as they were when the *Staroamer* left Earth. But they have another unpleasant quality that will work to your advantage: greed.

"Your science is worth a fortune. Use your inventions to trade. The artificial gravity alone could probably get you enough energy to use for a year. Maybe even decades. And this projection process—you can keep going on without worrying that the least wrong move would be the one little thing that means disaster."

"You make it sound tempting," Vorst said.

Quarnian smiled. She had found her lever; she was beginning to lift him free of his ruts. "That's the whole idea. You're too used to thinking the same way all the time. Try something different. All I ask is that you consider it; if you still think it's wrong for you, I promise you I *won't* tell anyone. But I think you can see it will be in the best interest of the *Staroamer*."

There was a short silence. "I'll think about it," Vorst said. He vanished, a pensive look on his face.

Quarnian looked at Rex. "Well, I suppose it's time to correct our course."

He smiled and began adjusting the controls.

*Quarnian, I . . . *

Quarnian turned to Sindona. *You'd better get out of the habit of mindspeaking. You're not going to get much chance to use it.*

I suppose.

And I want to tell you that I didn't mean to bring you through vacuum. But there seemed to be no other way.

I understand. I suppose I didn't really blame you; I was too panicked to think straight when I realized what happened. Besides, now we're even.

Even?

Vorst's time limit wasn't up when I said it was; we could still have gone back to the Staroamer. But I couldn't allow that. I'm sorry I risked your lives like that.

Quarnian began to laugh. *Look at us, apologizing all the time. We're safe now; I think we can agree to forget about it.*

"What are you two laughing at?" Rex asked.

"Nothing," Quarnian said, looking at Sindona; she was smiling, too. "Just a little joke."

"That looks like it," Rex reported. "We're headed for home."

Quarnian nodded. "How's the fuel holding out?"

"Well, we're not going to be able to land. But that's no problem; we can call for help as soon as we get near New Wichatah. We'll reach there in six weeks."

Quarnian looked over at Sindona. "How about gravity? Can we put some spin on the ship?"

"I'd have to figure it out. Why?"

"I think Sindona should have a chance to get used to it. There isn't much zero gee on New Wichatah."

Sindona propelled herself over at the mention of her name, arriving as Rex began punching numbers into the computer. "What's up?"

Rex looked at the figures. "Well, we can spare a little for that. Only half a gee, though."

"It'll do," Quarnian said.

Sindona nodded. "I've often wondered about living with gravity. It seems so . . . inconvenient, I guess."

Quarnian smiled. "Work on that, Rex. I could use having something solid under my feet after all this time."

A fourth figure joined them before he could touch the controls. "Quarnian?" Vorst asked.

Quarnian looked at Rex. "Our answer," she whispered. "Yes, Captain?"

"I've been trying for a half hour to find something wrong with your reasoning. I've failed. Go ahead and tell the worlds; we'll be ready for them."

"Thanks, Vorst. I know you'll be—"

"Yes, yes. I know. Do us a favor, though. We need more than power; we need people. We once talked about bringing more aboard. I know they won't be the best, but . . . you think you can persuade some to join us?"

Quarnian smiled. "No problem. You may even have to be selective."

"All right, then. Do that for us and we'll be happy. I'll be signing off now, but I have a message for you. Bruce wants me to say good-bye for him."

Quarnian took a moment to answer. "Tell him I say good-bye, too."

Rex's hand was on her arm. "Vorst, tell the little runt good-bye for me, too."

Quarnian looked at him. "Well, frast," he said, melting under her amused gaze, "he was part of the team."

"I'll pass along the messages," Vorst said. "And, if you ever want to visit us again, feel free. We won't try to keep you here. It's too difficult."

Quarnian smiled. "Thanks," she said as Vorst turned into empty space. She turned to Rex. "Let's have that gravity; I'm homesick already."

Chapter Twenty-four

Time passed more quickly than on the way out. Knowing their destination made the difference. New Wichatah wasn't the prettiest planet in the universe, but it looked just perfect as it got a tiny bit bigger each day.

They had moved mattresses from the cabins for a place to sleep. Sindona had locked herself in the head as they heated the airstone to make the entire cabin an airlock.

Quarnian was surprised how quickly Sindona adjusted to gravity. After two weeks, she walked as though she'd been doing it all her life. *It's no more tiring than weightlessness,* Sindona had thought.

Quarnian had smiled and warned her again that she should be talking out loud.

But there were other problems of adjustment. The ship's cabin seemed too small now that the three of them had no place else to go. Each of them had staked out an area of his or her own, but privacy was a problem. Quarnian sensed an undertone of uneasiness that she tried hard to dispel.

After three weeks of it, she heard her name in her mind just before they were all going to sleep.

*Sindona, I told you . . . *

Not right now. I want to be sure Rex doesn't hear us.

Quarnian sat up on her mattress, sighing. She wondered what the big secret was. *I don't want to keep anything from Rex.*

That's not why I'm doing this. I just wanted to tell you that I'm willing to pretend that I'm asleep if you want. There's no need to be embarrassed; I'm used to close quarters.

Quarnian looked over at her; she did appear to be sleeping. *What do you mean?*

If you and Rex want to get together for anything, I'll look the other way.

Get together? For what? But Quarnian knew what the answer was going to be: she felt her face becoming hot.

*Well, I know that you and him . . . *

You can forget about that. It was just because of the pheromones. Quarnian felt herself becoming more and more indignant.

There weren't any other times?

No, Quarnian replied.

Sindona projected a smile at her. *You're becoming a much better liar.*

Quarnian sighed. *All right. But that doesn't mean anything. Two people can make love together without it leading to anything more. I had sex with Taril, too.*

Because you wanted to?

No, Quarnian admitted. *But that had nothing . . . * She paused. Why was she arguing the point? *I don't want to talk about this anymore. You don't have to pretend anything.* She lay back down.

She was alone with her own indignant thoughts for several minutes. Then, suddenly, more words popped into her mind. *He loves you, Quarnian.*

What makes you—?

Oh, come on.

The overtones of the outburst quieted Quarnian for a minute. *OK. You're right. But that's his problem. We'll be going different ways once we get to New Wichatah. He'll just have to get over it. He's left other women before.*

Not like you.

Quarnian didn't bother with a reply. There was something presumptuous about Sindona's manner; it would be best to ignore her.

You love him, too, Sindona thought.

Quarnian fought the urge to laugh. That's what she was getting at! It was ludicrous—light-years wide of the mark. *Rex is a friend, that's all. But I don't love him.*

*Quarnian, you forget I can read your mind. You've been in love with him since I met you on the *Staroamer*. I noticed how you felt when he was trying to make a pass at me. Fact is, you had fallen in love with him even then.*

The urge to laugh suddenly vanished. *No, it's not . . . it can't be.*

Think. Think about how you feel about him. Right now. Think about leaving him.

She did. To her surprise, the thought was drenched in pain and regret. She'd miss Rex, miss him terribly.

You see?

Quarnian rubbed her face. *It can't be. I'm a syron.*

You're still human, aren't you? Let me let you in on a secret. Love is nice. Don't run away from it.

I have to. Quarnian had never felt this upset, even when she had given herself to other men. *My life's too up in the air. I can't make that sort of commitment. It'd never last.*

Relationships often don't.

All this silent conversation was upsetting Quarnian too much. *No,* she thought emphatically. *You're wrong. It sounds pretty, but it's just not true. I don't love Rex, and that's that.*

Quarnian could feel an emotion of neutrality coming from Sindona's mind, the equivalent of a shrug. *All right, suit yourself.* She stopped projecting.

Quarnian felt an odd relief that quickly gave way to indignation. Sindona had made a good case, but logic wasn't necessarily truth. Rex was a friend, a close one at that, but just a friend. They'd go their separate ways. He'd get over her; she'd forget about him by the time she reached her next stop.

Quarn? Sindona thought.

I told you I didn't like that nickname, Quarnian snapped, happy to have the chance to vent her anger on the person who caused it.

Oh? came the reply. *Rex calls you that all the time.*

Quarnian felt confused. *Yes, but that's because... because... * She couldn't finish the sentence.

Sindona did it for her. *Because he's different.* The words were filled with warm amusement. *Q.E.D. Welcome to the human race, Quarnian.*

You can't be much of a judge of that, Quarnian answered. The retort fell flat, the impetus behind it dissipated in self-reflection.

There was no further conversation, but Quarnian felt it hard to get to sleep.

Quarnian couldn't talk to Rex; their conversations were rare and only covered necessities. It was the best way, she had decided. There was no reason to tell what she had discovered. He'd get over her, she'd get over him.

A week from New Wichatah, they radioed for help.

"*Wreckless?*" The operator on the radio seemed amazed. "You're listed as missing; you're way overdue. Where have you been?"

Rex looked over at Quarnian.

"Well, go ahead," she said. "Tell him."

"He'll never believe us, you know."

"We've got evidence," Sindona broke in. "These clothes, me, the airstone..."

Rex nodded. "And those weapons."

Quarnian shook her head. "I don't want to be responsible for letting them get around. We'll keep the ones we have a secret."

Rex shrugged and picked up the mike. "You're not going to believe this, but..."

Evidently someone believed them; more than just the Planetary Patrol was waiting for them when they reached orbit.

"Looks like an armada," Rex commented.

Quarnian smiled. "That's the problem when you're

news." They had had to turn the radio off for the last three days; the requests for interviews and life stories were coming in every minute. She looked at Sindona. "Think you're ready to meet the media?"

"No." Sindona smiled. "But I'll manage."

"The reward will help."

"I suppose. Although I have no idea what I'll do with it."

Quarnian laughed. "You'll . . ." She stopped. There was something about Sindona's thought that struck her as strange. She glanced at Rex; he was busy maneuvering. *What's the matter?*

*I thought you said we weren't . . ."

Don't avoid the subject. Something's bothering you. What is it?

There was an amused overtone to Sindona's thought. *I guess we know each other too well; we can see each other's problems.*

Quarnian ignored the reference. *So tell me.*

That's just it; I can't seem to put a finger on it. Everything seems . . . empty. It's like . . . well, for as long as I can remember I've wanted to get away from the Staroamer. My escape was going to be the high point of my life. Now I'm past that and . . . I can't really express it.

The post-Christmas letdown.

What's that?

Quarnian explained.

Yes, Sindona thought. *But it's more than that. I feel . . . lost. I've never had many choices on the ship; now I have too many. I'm not sure I can adjust.*

Quarnian put her hand on her shoulder. *You will. Don't worry about it.*

I can't be an archivist; I doubt if there's any such occupation, anyway. Besides, I'm tired of history.

Look—

"If you two will stop that telepathy crap, we've got things to decide."

Quarnian felt herself turn red. "How did you . . . ?"

"You two looked like you were talking, even if I couldn't hear anything. Were you discussing me?"

Quarnian's embarassment got worse. "We didn't mean . . ."

"Don't worry about it, Rex," Sindona said. "Quarnian said only good things about you."

"It had nothing to do with you," Quarnian snapped, glaring at Sindona. *What are you trying to do?*

Just making things run smoothly between you two.

No one likes a matchmaker. I'm handling this the way I want it handled.

If you say so. "What sort of decisions do we have, Rex?"

"First of all, who do we let on board first?"

"I don't know about you," Sindona said, "but I'm tired of this cabin. We'll talk to everyone after we land. How's that sound, Quarnian?"

Quarnian grunted.

"Oh, stop being so annoyed." Sindona turned to Rex. "How about you?"

He nodded. "Sounds good. We'll talk later." He picked up the radio to announce their decision.

Events quickly became too hectic for introspection, or even for rational thought. Quarnian and Rex became instant legends, Sindona, a strange creature from a freak show of a society.

"Three offers for my life story," Sindona giggled. "It's bound to be the world's dullest entertainment."

"What one are you going to take?" Rex asked. The three of them were waiting outside the New Wichatah studios of the Centralized News Service; the Earth Heritage Society was going to present them with the reward for finding the lost ship.

Sindona shrugged. "I don't know. Maybe all, maybe none. You have any suggestions, Quarnian?"

"Just make sure it's cash up front," Quarnian said. "You're going to be a nine-day wonder; by the time anything's completed, you may find yourself washed up."

The waiting room was luxurious, like all their accommodations since their landing. There had been no shortage of people ecstatic to pick up the tab. Quarnian could sense their greed, a stench like that of rotting vegetables. She smiled; it wasn't likely Vorst was going to give away anything important. He was too frugal to be swindled.

The door opened and a balding young man, dressed in the tie that marked him as being from Earth, smiled his way into the room. "Hello, I'm Brian Wilfong. From the Society." He looked directly at Sindona. "You must be Quarnian Dow."

Sindona smiled and pointed him in the right direction.

"Ah, Ms. Dow. I'm sure you've heard that another ship has confirmed contact with the *Staroamer*."

It was news to her, but Quarnian nodded anyway.

"Then I can safely tell you the money is yours."

"Just how much money are we talking about?" Rex asked.

"I have the draft right here." Wilfong patted his pocket. "In local currency, it comes to twenty-five thousand trents."

"Twenty-five thousand?" Rex asked. "I thought it would be more."

"That was all the Atkinsons donated to the *Staroamer* discovery fund. I don't know how much you know about them. It seems their two sons had both been chosen . . ."

"Just a minute," Rex interrupted. "Hasn't that money been earning any interest? It's been centuries."

Wilfong looked at the floor. "I'm afraid . . ."

"You robbed us!" Rex shouted. He advanced on the Society representative. "What have you done with our money?"

Wilfong retreated. "It *was* earning interest, that's true. But over the years . . . well, the Society has expenses, you know." He took another step back. "The Atkinsons only stipulated the twenty-five thousand to be used and . . . well, to be frank, no one really believed the *Staroamer* would ever be found." Rex had nearly backed him into a corner. "Well," he said, his voice becoming somewhat squeaky, "I think I'll go see if everything's ready."

Wilfong disappeared through the door he had entered.

Quarnian and Sindona began to laugh.

Rex turned slowly, his face glaring. Then, bit by bit, it began to soften, melted into a smile by their laughter. "I suppose it *did* look funny," he admitted. He began to laugh, too.

The New Yorker restaurant was an attempt to recreate the charm of that old Earth city at its height. Sindona had suggested the meal there; Quarnian could sense she had more on her mind than eating.

She gave no hint, and just smiled when Quarnian tried to question her.

"That was good," Sindona said when the steak and potatoes had vanished from her plate. "I always wondered what meat tasted like. I can see why it caught on."

"What are you being so mysterious about?" Rex asked.

Quarnian looked at him. So he saw through it, too.

Sindona held up a hand. "Please. If I can't announce this the way I want, you'll take all the fun out of it. I just want to tell you two a few things."

Quarnian felt a sudden tenseness. Sindona was going to ruin everything, tell Rex what she knew about Quarnian's feelings. She'd never be able to extricate herself from him easily then. "Like what?"

"Well, I was wondering what you two are going to do with your rewards."

Rex snorted.

Sindona smiled. "It's better than nothing. How about it, Rex?"

"How about you?"

"No fair. It's my question."

Rex was silent as he seemed to think. His eyes stayed on Sindona as though he was wondering if she would press him. Evidently the answer was yes. "I don't know. I had expected to do much better. I guess my share will be almost enough to pay off the mortgage on the *Wreckless,* though."

Quarnian frowned. "You don't seem too happy about that."

"It's all right." Rex shrugged. "I just expected something more." He stared at Quarnian; the gaze made her feel uncomfortable. "I had hoped I might at least hit a big enough jackpot to install warp drive. It's tough to make a living on a single-system run."

Quarnian couldn't miss the overtone of disappointment in the way he spoke. She had cheated him, she knew, both emotionally and financially. She looked down at her empty plate. One couldn't be helped; it was the nature of things. But the other... "Rex... if you like, you can have my share."

"You don't have to..."

She knew his protest was halfhearted. "I don't need most of it—just enough to get me to my next destination."

"Where's that?" Sindona asked.

The question surprised Quarnian. "I don't know yet. I haven't thought much about it. Anyway, Rex, I'd like you to have it. All but, say, eight hundred trents. For the trouble I caused you."

"It was no trouble."

"Rex," Sindona said, "take the money before she comes to her senses."

Rex smiled. "All right. You two ladies win. But it still won't be enough to add warp drive."

"That's where I can help," Sindona said.

Quarnian shook her head. "That's crazy. You'll need the money to live on. All these offers are going to dry up very soon. It may be some time before you find something to do."

"I've already decided. I'll just keep enough to pay for a passage to Earth. I'm going to become a syron."

The words hung in the air.

Quarnian was the one who snapped the silence. "You're crazy. You know what I have to go through. Why would you—"

"Quarnian, you know you love being a syron."

"But I have no choice in anything. I have to—"

"You've been singing that same old song for a long time. I know there'll be bad times. But tell me the truth. Aren't you proud of most everything you've done?"

Quarnian couldn't answer. She had never thought of it that way. All that seemed to stick in her mind was the hardships, the worry, and the pain. If there was more than that, she rarely considered it.

"I don't know," she said very quietly. "I really don't."

Sindona leaned back. "Well, I do. I've already contacted

the Institute. I'm going to begin the Training as soon as I get to Earth."

"Just a minute," Rex said. "That doesn't mean anything. You may not be any good at it."

"Don't worry, Rex. I will be. I'll be a gold star."

"What makes you so sure?"

Sindona looked at Rex, then at Quarnian. She smiled. "Call it a hunch."

After the celebration, Sindona left for another interview. Quarnian felt like being alone, so she wandered through the city, her thoughts her only companion.

She had begun to sniff the air to pick up the hunch that would lead her to her next destination, but nothing came. She was as void of intuition as she had been during her depression on the *Staroamer*.

She wondered if she was losing her gold-star status; it had happened to others. She'd end up like the pawnshop dealer who had recognized her so long before. It would be a relief to be human again, she thought. I'd like to have the illusion I was my own pilot.

At other times, the thought would have cheered her. Tonight, it didn't.

She found that she had returned to the spaceport. Tired of wandering, she walked slowly to the *Wreckless*.

The sound of laughter snapped her out of her thoughts. She glanced up and saw Rex. He was almost to the entrance to the ship. Beside him was a red-haired woman.

Quarnian froze.

But it was too late. The woman had turned and then pointed at her. Rex nodded in grudging acknowledgement and they began to walk toward her.

"You're Quarnian Dow," the woman said. She was short and quite pretty. "I recognized you right away."

Quarnian somehow managed to smile and make conversation. She kept glancing at Rex. He seemed both ashamed and defiant at the same time.

The woman must have sensed some of the tension. "Well, we won't keep you. Rex is going to show me the *Wreckless*."

From the tone of her voice, Quarnian knew she was anticipating more than just a tour.

Rex hung back as she headed off, as though expecting
Quarnian to say something.

No, Quarnian realized. He *wanted* her to say something.
She realized he knew her feelings about him, that he had
known for some time. And she understood with total clarity
that the right words from her could make a world of difference. All she had to do was forget she was a syron. . . .

"Coming, Rex?" the woman called.

And Quarnian spoke. "Enjoy yourself, Rex. Sindona and
I will stay somewhere else tonight."

A wall of silence surrounded them. Then Rex spoke. "Too
bad," he murmured, the words an acceptance of the inevitable. They were filled with sadness and regret—and with
understanding.

"It's best," Quarnian whispered.

"I wish you weren't right."

"Rex, how long have you known? About the way I felt."

"When you first offered to make love with me." He
grinned. "Scared the hell out of me."

"Rex?" the waiting redhead asked.

He shook his head, then brightened. "We never *did* say
we loved each other."

Quarnian smiled. "No. We never did. Go on, Rex. Your
next conquest awaits."

Rex grinned and walked away.

Quarnian's prediction was correct. After two more weeks,
they were pushed off the headlines by the report of another
alien race discovered by a syron near Dubhe. The excitement over, Sindona saw no reason to stay any longer. Quarnian was with her as she waited for the liner to Earth.

"Where's Rex?" Sindona asked her.

"He . . . he couldn't make it."

"Didn't want to say good-bye, huh? I'm flattered. I guess
he doesn't want to risk getting emotional."

"That, plus I think he has plans to entertain a visitor.
Female, of course." Quarnian was pleased to realize the

smile on her lips was genuine. "He told me I could take my time coming back."

Sindona shook her head. "You know, if you told him—"

"I know. He'd drop her like a hot meteorite. But I'm not telling him."

"But, why not? You can stay together—especially since the *Wreckless* will soon be a warship."

Quarnian grinned. "So *that's* why you were so generous. But it still won't work."

"Relationships sometimes don't."

"But this is different. How long do you think Rex and I could work as equals? One of us would have to dominate. Probably me, since I have all sorts of tricks he can't use. How long would he stand for that? Or what happens the next time I have to sleep with a stranger to accomplish something? Or manipulate him just to get my way?" She shook her head. "There are a hundred reasons why we'd only end up hating each other violently. No. Sometimes the best way to love someone is to leave him. At least that way we can still be friends." Quarnian smiled. "I know, deep down, that Rex understands that."

Sindona didn't speak for a moment; then she sighed. "Can't blame me for trying."

"I don't." Quarnian looked down the terminal. People were rushing to make it to the gate. "You'd better go. Wouldn't want the Institute's star pupil to be late."

Sindona smiled. "I'm not sure I'll be *that* good."

"You'd *better* be—after what I went through to recruit you."

Sindona laughed. "Well, I just hope I'm half as good as you."

"This mutual admiration is getting disgusting. Good-bye, Sindona."

"Good-bye, Quarnian." Sindona turned and walked toward the departure gate to the shuttle that would take her to her warp liner.

Quarnian watched her vanish inside. There was no sadness. She had a hunch their paths would cross again.

She stayed only long enough to see Sindona's ship lift off. As it vanished from sight, she headed for the exit.

What now? she thought. She had no plans for the next few hours.

She saw the ticket counter, and her eyes were caught by it. It gave her a funny feeling, strange, yet totally familiar. . . .

Quarnian walked up to the clerk. He looked at her and then smiled. "Yes?"

Before she could consider it, a question came to mind. "Where's your next liner going?"

If the question surprised him, he gave no sign. "The *Marzetti* leaves in seventeen minutes. Goes to Gemma, Argus, Princia, and Delespoir. From there you . . ."

But Quarnian wasn't listening to the rest. One name glowed in the air like a miniature moon, its sound sending chills of anticipation through her. "Delespoir," she said. "How much for passage?"

The amount she had set aside was just enough. Of course. In a few minutes, she had booked passage.

She glanced at the time. She could just call Rex, tell him she was leaving. . . .

She shook her head. Rex would not be answering. And, anyway, he'd guess the reason for her abrupt departure. He knew she was a syron.

Quarnian's hand touched her pendant. Its tiny weight felt very comforting. Humming a song, she hurried to catch the *Marzetti*.